# Temptation

16

# Temptation

## Dermot Bolger

**Flamingo**
*An Imprint of* HarperCollins*Publishers*

Flamingo
An Imprint of HarperCollins*Publishers*
77–85 Fulham Palace Road,
Hammersmith, London w6 8jb

www.**fire**and**water**.com

Flamingo is a registered trade mark of HarperCollins*Publishers* Limited

Published by Flamingo 2000
1 3 5 7 9 8 6 4 2

Copyright © Dermot Bolger 2000

Dermot Bolger asserts the moral right to be identified
as the author of this work

This novel is entirely a work of fiction. The names, characters and
incidents portrayed in it are the work of the author's imagination. Any
resemblance to actual persons, living or dead, is entirely coincidental.
Its location however is inspired by Kelly's Resort Hotel, Rosslare,
Co Wexford, run by the family of that name for over a century.

A catalogue record for this book
is available from the British Library

ISBN 0 00 226152 9

Set in Postscript Bembo by Rowland Phototypesetting Ltd,
Bury St Edmunds, Suffolk

Printed and bound in Great Britain by
Clays Ltd, St Ives plc

*For Edwin Higel*

# SUNDAY

I gave up my happiness to make another person happy, Alison thought, for the briefest half-conscious second when she woke beside Peadar in the night. I was somebody else once, someone different. Why was she thinking this? Their packed bags and suitcases lined the bedroom wall although she couldn't see their shapes in the dark. Tomorrow Peadar would stack them in the car as usual. What was the dream she was trying to block out? At first all she could remember was water, a tang of salt on her lips, fear, the excitement of being somebody else. The vaguest sexual thrill. Then darkness.

But another image forced itself into her mind, from later in the dream or perhaps from a different one. An image so terrifying that she wanted to wake Peadar. A woman's face under water, trapped at the window of a capsized boat. Skeletal, the flesh half gone, bony hands upright where they had beat against the glass. Eyes that had not yet been devoured, staring out, watching as a tiny capsule approached. Its headlights picking up the rusted hull in the mud, the drifting seaweed, the huge eyes of striped flatfish. Except that Alison knew she wasn't in the tiny submarine. It was she who was trapped in the wreckage and her wrists that had bruised themselves against the glass, her sagging breasts that protruded through the tattered dress, her veins that stood out like blue highways criss-crossing a desert.

She was afraid to close her eyes again now, frightened the image would return. Yet, even with her eyes wide open in the dark, every detail remained clear. Her right nipple half eaten away by some dark sea creature. She felt that breast now, almost smooth underneath again where the single stitch had healed. She ran her hand over the nipple which, ever since the touch of Dr O'Gorman's hand, no longer felt like hers. Peadar still sleepily reached for it some mornings, like a child instinctively seeking a battered toy he had outgrown. But did he ever look at them properly any more, the breasts of his thirty-eight-year-old wife? If he did, then surely he would have noticed something.

Alison hated these insidious three a.m. thoughts, demanding answers to questions she had no desire to ask. Like how had she come to be here, at this age, in this bed, beside this man? She loved Peadar and there was nowhere else she wanted to be, so why did the eyes of that woman haunt her from the dream? All her own wishes had come true. She had never longed to explore the Nile or cross the Andes. If she could have looked ahead at twenty-one to see herself now, then surely she would have been pleased. Owning a house in Raheny, the sight of which had awed her parents into silence, having three children who loved her and a successful husband who still looked boyish in a certain light.

At twenty-one she had been convinced she would end up alone. That loneliness, or the aching remembrance of it, had never left her. Walking out one Sunday over the rough stones of the Pigeon House wall, a tall figure huddled up in a coat and wearing a monkey hat against the rain, hoping against hope there might be a coffee shop at the end of the pier, somewhere out of the cold, friendly and anonymous, where some stranger might talk to her.

She could never have understood back then how there might be other kinds of loneliness even when living inside a family. This three a.m. isolation. Not that Peadar had ever stopped loving her, but sometimes he forgot how much reassurance she needed. At thirty-eight, a body changes. He had to sense it too. Was it his own ageing which caused him to always come so quickly of late or was it a lack of sustained interest in her? Twenty years ago he had been so stiff with over-excitement that he often barely seemed able to come. Now at times their lovemaking felt like a habit without need of speech, an instinctive curling into safe, established positions, his arm routinely around her as they slipped towards shared sleep.

But was it shared? What was Peadar dreaming about with such laboured breath and was she a part of it? Sixteen years of marriage, twenty years of intimacy, even if they had remained apart for three of them. Surely Alison should know him by now, surely she should feel secure? Perhaps that was the problem, they were too secure. How could she really know who Peadar was, when often at three a.m. Alison didn't even know who she herself was, buried inside the bustle and happiness of her family life.

Peadar slept on, curled up inside dreams that, Alison decided, most probably concerned bricks and mortar. Peadar the planner, desperate to leave a mark behind. But tomorrow was holiday time, the five carefree nights she had been living out for months in advance. So why did she feel fearful, with a sense of foreboding souring her stomach? Those eyes still swayed in the dark above her, a tang of salt on her lips, a sense of water ebbing invisibly across the sheets, rocking her back into dreams that belonged to someone else.

———— ❧ ————

All year they talked about it. It even defined them with some friends, people they wouldn't see for months on end, but who always greeted them with the same remark, 'So tell us, are you going to Fitzgerald's again this year?'

The remark – it wasn't really a question any more – came to annoy Alison. It made them seem staid and middle-aged before their time. Later, in the car home, she might argue with Peadar about going camping in France or visiting Barcelona like they'd done the summer after they married. But even as she railed against his stock list of excuses about the children being too small and language problems, Alison knew that Peadar could sense she was merely going through the motions, even if he gave no sign of understanding what caused her malaise.

In truth Alison *was* growing staid and middle-aged. Thirty-eight. Twenty years ago how ancient and decrepit that would have seemed. Twenty years ago she would have laughed at the annual notion of five nights in Fitzgerald's Hotel during the second week of Peadar's Easter school holidays. Twenty years ago she could never have imagined that one day she might afford to regularly stay there.

The three children woke her at seven-thirty as usual that Sunday morning by climbing into bed to demand a cuddle. The two boys were barely in before they wriggled free, asking to be allowed to watch children's television. Their hot, bony limbs clambered off the mattress and she heard doors bang downstairs and the television being plugged in. Five-year-old Sheila snuggled on, spooning into her as Peadar slowly stirred. He turned to kiss Alison and stroke Sheila's hair, then swung his legs from the bed. Mr Action Man, ready to organise them. Alison lay on, enjoying her daughter's soft skin as Sheila played with the ragdoll she had decided to bring to Fitzgerald's. But something lingered, the fragment of a dream that perturbed Alison without her being able to fully recall its details. Just eyes under water, shredded flesh.

She shuddered briefly in the warm morning light, hugged Sheila tight and pushed the image away. Sheila was walking the ragdoll up along the quilt, until it perched on Alison's nose, staring down at her eyes.

'Get up, lazybones, we're going on holidays,' a squeaky voice demanded.

Peadar moved about downstairs, doing his drill master sergeant impersonation. This was the first year when loading the car wouldn't prove a near impossible logistical feat. Previously he would spend an eternity in the driveway, getting increasingly flustered as he rearranged their bags, shouting at the boys if they wandered out, half dressed and wanting the adventure to start. This year – with Sheila sleeping in a bed and the battered travel cot and buggy no longer required – their luggage would fit first time. But Alison knew, as she heard the rattle of her breakfast tray being carried upstairs, that Peadar would take the bags down as soon as he'd laid the tray on the bed. Loading the car first thing seemed as much a part of Peadar's holiday ritual as her surprise breakfast in bed, his way of trying to leave the frantic pace of his everyday world behind.

She called out for him to leave the boys' bag alone as she had more clothes to pack. He put it down reluctantly, like a child denied a final piece of jigsaw. They wouldn't leave for another hour, yet she knew he wouldn't be happy until the boot was shut for a final time.

Sheila slid out of bed and padded down after Peadar, saying that she wanted him to get her dressed. Alison was pleased, knowing this would buy her more time. Why did he always have to make their departure to Fitzgerald's so rushed? Normally she was so wound up by the time they reached there that they had an argument on the first night.

This year was the first time they had ever seriously considered cancelling. Their fitted kitchen was already antiquated when they had moved into the house ten years ago and was now completely falling apart. Over Christmas Alison had argued that they should get a new kitchen instead of taking a holiday. Finances were tight since she'd given up nursing, even on Peadar's salary as a school principal. But although, in the end, she had claimed to have chosen Fitzgerald's so as not to disappoint the children, in reality it was the prospect of this holiday which had sustained her during the secrecy of these last months.

She ate quickly now, going over endless lists in her head. Danny still got sick when he travelled and needed Phenergan medicine before they started. Tapes had to be organised in advance: songs and rhymes that Sheila would enjoy, over the others' protests, until she fell asleep, and then a cassette of stories for seven-year-olds, carefully pitched in age between Danny and Shane. In previous years they would all fall asleep, leaving Peadar and her free to drive in silence past Enniscorthy, feeling the road widen as she silently crossed off the miles. Now their voices would fill the car all the way to Fitzgerald's.

Shouts rose from downstairs – Danny teasing Shane, Shane being hypersensitive. Tears and blows were only moments away. She abandoned the remains of her breakfast and made for the stairs, pitching her tone somewhere between that of a UN peacemaker and a wounded benign dictator.

———— ৵ ————

The children always started counting down the miles before they'd even left Dublin. One hundred and one exactly from their driveway to the hotel car park. Peadar drove. In the early years she had shared the driving, just to show that she was not dependent. Peadar had known better than to complain but she had sensed his eyes checking the speed gauge, humouring her for the time they were losing. Peadar didn't think of himself as a fast driver, but claimed that the N11 was a road you needed to know. There were stretches where you drove slowly and others where you clawed back the lost time. Perhaps it was the pressures of his job, the endless timetables, crises and fundraising targets, which made him live his life against some invisible clock. But this year Alison planned to let him get on with driving, knowing that he hated the purposelessness of being a passenger. Peadar's idea of a holiday, she often thought, would be two weeks in old jeans being useful with a Black and Decker drill. That, plus afternoon sex, kicking a football with Danny and Shane, sketching out a few projects for the future and the occasional round of golf thrown in.

He simply had to drive by the school, of course, even though it wasn't on their way. Peadar half glanced across at her, wondering if he dared to stop. Beyond the boundary wall, scaffolding rose around what would soon be the finished extension. One night, after Peadar came in at two a.m. from doing budgets with McCann, his vice-principal, he had promised to let Alison smash a bottle of champagne against the finished extension to open it. She was only half joking when she'd threatened to smash himself and McCann on a rope against it instead.

He slowed the car, almost imperceptibly, his eyes following the contractor's workmen who were earning double time for a Sunday. She could sense him gauging, almost to the brick, how far behind schedule they were with the school due to reopen in eight days.

Four years of his life were ground up in the mortar of that extension, four years of lost evenings and weekends. Nobody else could have done it on such a tiny grant, wheedling money here and there, organising bag-packing at local supermarkets, sponsored walks, Christmas vigil fasts, read-a-thons, cultivating politicians and local clergy who still harboured suspicions about multi-denominational schools. In bed at night Alison used to tease him about strategies he hadn't tried yet: sponsored hand-jobs outside pubs at closing time from the female teachers, kidnapping, extortion, strip poker sessions during the Parents Association nights, a declaration of war against the United States followed by a Marshall Plan appeal for rebuilding. But mostly she felt proud of him, even if she occasionally allowed herself to acknowledge a silent, mutinous resentment. This was generally followed by guilt, as she could never decide if her pique stemmed from the intrusion of his plans into their everyday world or because he made her own life, by contrast, seem lacking in purpose or direction.

The car slowed to a halt as if Peadar was reluctant to tear his eyes from the workmen.

'Only seven have bothered showing up,' he said. 'There should be a crew of eight working this morning.'

Danny leaned forward, making such a threatening noise that Peadar pulled away. Alison smiled, glad she had said nothing. It was hard to know what Danny would be in later life, but Alison wouldn't be surprised if he became a contract killer specialising in architects.

After the Shankill by-pass the stop-start prevarication of traffic lights ended. It was open road from here to the outskirts of Ashford. Not that the route was easy – it still narrowed to one lane passing Kilmacanoge and through the Glen of the Downs, with huge container trucks straining to get past to reach the ferry to France at Rosslare.

Her Aunt Catherine had grown up in a cottage perched above this road, cycling to school in Bray during the war, fetching water from a green pump a half mile away. Alison still found herself watching out for the cottage, refurbished now and almost unrecognisable as the insignificant building pointed out to her as a child, since it had gained a conservatory and electronic gates. During their early years of driving to Fitzgerald's she would show it to Peadar until she had grown tired of retelling the story. Now it was Peadar who drew her attention to it, every year on the same bend, like a talisman in their ritual.

The habit annoyed her, yet she would have been disappointed if he had let the moment pass. This was part of being thirty-eight too, finding that life had developed into certain grooves that made you feel secure. There were a dozen tiny habits of Peadar that irritated her, yet none of which she would change. It was like the leaking tap in the shed he had been meaning to fix for so long. She would miss the company of its drip now, putting in a wash down there at night or giving the uniforms a five-minute midnight tumble in the dryer before leaving them out for the morning.

Peadar with a perpetual tuft of hair in his nostril, the first part of him to go grey. Peadar like a furnace beside her in the bed, grumbling if she kicked off the spare blanket he kept on his side in winter even when obviously unneeded. Peadar who had never lost his Galway accent. Peadar at the beck and call of parents and neighbours during the few hours he was at home. Alison would be suspicious of some of the women calling if she didn't know that he hadn't got it in him to be unfaithful, no matter what her friend Ruth said about all men being the same. Peadar the builder, the planner. Peadar who had taken that Mickey Mouse school by the scruff of the neck. Peadar who was her rock in any storm. Peadar who had stoically watched his mother succumb to Alzheimer's during monthly visits home to Galway, until she finally asked the nurse to make the strange man go away. Peadar who, since her death, hurt Alison sometimes by clamming up in his makeshift office upstairs, as if possessed by a growing malady that not even he could fathom. Peadar from whom she had kept the secret of these last few months.

Sheila was asleep before the car slowed on the narrow road twisting through woodland slopes into Ashford. They would have to wake her now when they reached Mount Ussher Gardens and the child might grow cranky later in the journey. Danny was quiet. Last year he would have prattled away until he fell asleep, pointing out passing tractors to the stuffed giraffe he once took everywhere with him. He still cuddled into that tattered giraffe after bedtime stories and sometimes stumbled into their room at night, half asleep, upset that his beloved toy had fallen behind the bed. But Alison knew this was the last year the giraffe would make the journey to Fitzgerald's.

She had told him not to read in the car but Danny had taken out the *Shoot* football magazine which he now ordered in the newsagent's instead of his Batman comic. He was intently studying match reports of obscure English third division games. She could see their names highlighted in the dense text on the page he had turned over. Southend, Doncaster, Brentford, teams and towns that could have no meaning for him. Yet his eyes seemed mesmerised, absorbed in a foreign language that took him further and further away from her. Danny, her firstborn, a gentle child never quite fitting in anywhere but happy to hover on the edge of some horde of boys. How much longer before he stopped climbing into her bed for a dawn cuddle? But he still needed her and would for a long time to come. That's why she had to be here for him and for them all. That's why, during the previous three months, she had been too scared to talk to anyone.

'I know what happened, Mammy,' six-year-old Shane had informed her recently as she pushed him on a swing. 'Danny must have fallen at school and banged his head. That's why he started liking football.' Shane had swung his feet in the air, satisfied at solving the mystery of his brother's conversion to soccer and, with it, his abandonment of the endless games of Batman and Robin he'd once devised for them both.

Shane was more babyish than Danny had been at that age but tougher as well. He'd always known his own mind. Danny was malleable, but even at a few hours old when Alison had put Shane to feed at her breast she'd felt a resistance in his neck. She'd let him go and his tiny mouth had found her nipple by itself. Shane would grow up in his own time as his own man, with nothing to prove to anybody. For now he clutched his Paddington Bear proudly in the car and would refuse to eat everything except bread when they reached Mount Ussher Gardens.

The car park just beyond Ashford was on a dangerous bend. You were almost past before you saw the entrance. A German camper van was leaving. Peadar eased into the free space and she cautioned the boys against jumping out with so many cars about. Peadar got them out and put their coats on. Sheila was sleeping so peacefully that Alison was tempted to tell them to go ahead while she remained in the car until the child woke. But something – the engine being turned off or the shudder made by the slipstream of a truck thundering past – caused Sheila's eyes to open. Danny would fly into a rage and sometimes get sick if woken, but Sheila just smiled now as if delighted to see her mother anxiously leaning over her.

Alison unstrapped her. Peadar and the boys had already

passed the antique shops. Stopping at Mount Ussher was part of the ritual too, the midway point between Dublin and Wexford when she could finally relax. A week of preparation went into these five nights away. Washing, sorting clothes, packing. It always took longer than expected, with Peadar hovering while she frantically crossed things off her list and their tempers flared up.

In previous years the journey to this point was spent wondering what had she left behind, if the windows were double-locked or the alarm definitely on. But this year felt different. Suddenly she didn't care if the house burnt down when they were away. At least the battered kitchen would have to be replaced then.

The sun emerged after a squall of rain. Everything glistened as she walked, holding Sheila's hand, beneath the archway of climbing plants to the tea rooms. The air felt like a benediction: the wet leaves, the excited laughter from her sons, the trees swaying in the gardens beyond. In January, when Dr O'Gorman's cold hand had examined her breast, Alison had felt sure she would never stand here again, except as a dying woman or one scarred for life.

Why had she never told Peadar? She would tomorrow night, sipping complimentary Irish coffees on the long sofas in Fitzgerald's. He would take her hand, near tears, and scold her for not having spoken. He would not trivialise it by going over the details repeatedly. She liked the clear-cut way that he absorbed information. He would ask one or two questions then lapse into silence, squeezing her hand before suggesting they return to the room. Holding hands, they would walk up the long corridor, where a baby always cried behind some door, and pay the babysitter off early. Their lovemaking would be silent so as not to wake the children, but with an edge caused by the knowledge of how fragile their world together was. Finally and fully she would have his attention.

She had been right to carry the dead weight of this worry alone. The weeks of waiting would have gnawed at Peadar. He would have hated the powerlessness of being unable to do anything, just like he had dreaded having to watch impotently while Alzheimer's drained away his mother's personality. Fear would have come between them, cancer taken possession of the house, filling their dreams and waking thoughts. In some lost fragment of his childhood, which she had learnt never to intrude upon, she was sure that his terror at not being in control was born.

But although in January she had been concerned about the tiny lump on the underside of her breast, she had expected reassurance from Dr O'Gorman and confirmation that it was just a cyst. Instead he had insisted on a mammogram. The public waiting list was months long. It was simpler to go privately, using the children's allowance money she kept in a separate account. She was a nurse herself she'd informed the radiographer: he could tell her straight out. But people's attitudes changed once they realised you had left nursing to work as a stay-at-home mother. She'd had to return to Dr O'Gorman, who would make Eeyore the donkey seem cheerful. He had insisted that the only way to ensure the cyst was benign was to remove it.

Even then, in mid March, she never told Peadar. She had lied instead on the morning of the procedure, claiming that she was going to help out Ruth, whose marriage had broken up, by staying with her overnight. The operation was in the same hospital she'd worked in. They had treated her like royalty – in at nine a.m., woken in mid-afternoon to be told the cyst was benign and sent home in time to read stories to Sheila. She couldn't stop trembling in the taxi, released from the scenario where she would have to tell Peadar how her breast was to be removed and that, even then, they didn't know how far the cancer had spread.

Instead she simply told him that Ruth hadn't needed her to stay over. She had hoped he wouldn't want to make love because of the soreness, but, during the previous months Peadar had never even noticed the small cyst develop, never mind now become aware of the tiny neat stitch on the underside. Lately he was too preoccupied in his world of contractors and architects. It hurt her when he barely noticed how much weight she had lost since Christmas, how pale she had looked or how red her eyes were at times.

When he did notice anything, it was to accuse her of sulking, being grudging in her support when he needed it most. He knew that he wasn't pulling his weight at home, he would say, but the school extension was almost built. Just these final crucial weeks and then the damn thing would be finished. An achievement nobody had thought possible. After that he'd be at home so much that she would grow sick of him. So why this long face and brooding, he would ask, just now when he'd so much to cope with? Then always, as if promising a child a treat, he would add, 'And remember, we'll have five whole nights to ourselves in Fitzgerald's.'

Five nights. Was this all her life boiled down to? On a dozen occasions she had bitten her tongue, tempted to scream at him. Yet these five nights would make up for so much. This scare would bring them closer together, by reminding them how some day – hopefully not for decades yet – one of them would be left to cope alone. All the bricks and mortar in the world couldn't compensate for closing a front door at night and knowing there was no one left to really care whether or not you woke again the next morning.

If the children weren't with them Alison might have told Peadar now on that secluded bench in the gardens overlooking the Ventry river where they had made love late one rainy afternoon sixteen years before. Alison, with the tear that Peadar had found in her skirt, sitting astride him with his flies undone. Thankfully not even the gardeners were moving about that day, but by the end they wouldn't have stopped or cared. Their excitement had been addictive, the feel of him thrusting through the material, the creak of an old beech tree overhead, the dark river gushing over rocks and a solitary heron taking flight before their eyes. The gardens were closing by the time they had left, with just their bicycles in the car park. Her dress was stained but she hadn't cared. She had cared about nothing that summer, except that she was twenty-two and free, on a dirty weekend with her first love who had come back after three years to find her.

Peadar was already ordering food in the tea rooms. The old lady in the hunting jacket was in her usual place beside the antiques, guarding the door into the gardens. Three local women ran the tea room. They remembered Peadar because of his fondness for rhubarb streusel. Danny was eyeing the rich cakes, but once they had a good walk it was unlikely he would get sick later on in the car. Alison scanned the menu, wondering was there anything she could persuade Shane to taste. Maybe she could invent a game to coax him into trying chicken. She envied women whose sons ate like horses. Yet Shane was tall and healthy, existing mainly on milk and cheese.

None of this was important, she reminded herself, or at least not at this moment. Let Shane drink what he likes. Let Danny have two cakes or three. Childhood was short and her own seemed to have been spent forever gazing in through invisible windows, being denied the things she saw inside and made to feel guilty for even wanting them. Not that her parents were mean, but the Waterford she grew up in had felt like it was ruled by some headscarfed matriarch with pursed, disapproving lips. It was a different world for children now. They were a family together on the sort of holiday she had only ever known once as a child. She had survived her scare, even if for days after getting the all-clear she had burst into sudden inexplicable tears, alone in the kitchen.

Peadar glanced at her now as the lady filled his tray.

'You look flushed,' he said. 'Are you okay?'

'I'm fine,' she replied. 'Just fine.'

The woman mashed up potatoes, carrots and gravy for Sheila and heated them in the microwave. Even with coaxing, the child would only eat half of it but there was enough goodness in that. Alison had plain biscuits wrapped in tissue for afterwards. She knew that both Sheila and Shane would enjoy them far more than any dessert.

The children stormed out into the gardens after they'd finished, while Peadar was still paying the admission fee. The azaleas were in bloom, stretching out before her eyes in pinks, yellows and whites as Alison walked through maple trees towards the river. Parts of the grass were deliberately cut long to give the woodlands a feel of half wilderness, half exotic Eden. Peadar appeared behind her, taking her hand but urging her on, anxious not to lose sight of Shane as the boy climbed up rough steps to a suspension bridge leading to the owner's house located on a man-made island in the river. Alison called for Shane to run after Danny and Sheila who had disappeared among the trees. She wanted to stroll in peace with Peadar along the wide avenue of hanging rhododendrons.

There was an octagonal wooden house at the end where she remembered changing Danny, the first year they went to Fitzgerald's, when everything was new and she was frantic about being a mother. The fear she might drop him, the incessant worry that caused her to wake several times a night to check his breathing in the cot.

Danny now gripped Sheila's hand as he pushed ahead towards the shallow stretch of river, hoping to see the solitary heron there again this year. Another talisman of their journey. Even at eight the boy was caught up in this ritual. The riverbed was empty. Danny cupped his hand over his eyes, straining to glimpse the bird. She called out that the heron was probably hunting along the far rapids and Danny disappeared across the bridge into a tunnel of old overhanging trees.

Shane followed, running along the maze of woodland paths, while Peadar called for them not to get lost. She let go of Peadar's hand, tired of being hurried, wanting to enjoy the cool shade of those gnarled trunks. Her family moved ahead, with Sheila demanding that Peadar carry her. From Danny's cries she knew he had found the entrance to the secret path built along girders down a tiny tributary of the river. The steps descended to the water, with ferns and moss crowding the steep banks on either side. Sheila was frightened of falling in and wriggled away to run back to Alison.

She sat on the grass with her daughter, watching Peadar hold each boy's hand as they negotiated their way slowly along the girders that were almost submerged in the green water. They disappeared in and out of shade, with patches of sunlight igniting the ripples that sparkled around them. This was a moment she knew she would remember when they were all gone from her. The three men in her life, calling excitedly to each other as they stooped beneath archways and rocks. Then their voices went silent, as if the riot of trailing plants along the riverbank had somehow ensnared them up inside a magical green world.

---

Peadar's car-phone rang as they descended the twisty mountain road beyond Rathnew, stuck behind a horsebox being pulled by a jeep in a tailback of Sunday afternoon vehicles. Alison thought he had remembered to turn it off. He glanced across, with a sheepish grin. She knew he couldn't resist picking it up.

'Just once,' she warned him. 'If it rings again it's going out the window.'

It was McCann, of course, fretful and over-conscientious as usual. Alison had grown to dread his voice calling at ridiculous hours about trivial matters. At first she had thought this was his method of retribution against Peadar for taking the principal's job that outsiders felt he had patiently waited in

F69, 866

line for, during his decade as vice-principal, before Peadar was headhunted for the post. But gradually she'd realised that his obsequiousness was without irony or malice. McCann was a natural lieutenant, not a leader. He lived alone, with classical music always in the background when he phoned, seemingly oblivious to the disruption caused by a midnight call.

'I know,' she heard Peadar say. 'I passed the site. There were seven then . . . maybe another two have bunked off. But the deadline is in place with penalty clauses, so they'll just have to work longer in the evenings.'

There was a silence as Peadar let McCann fret on. The secret was to wait until McCann paused for breath and then get your goodbyes in fast. Peadar braked as the horsebox slowed even more.

'If he's got three sites going at once then that's Nolan's problem,' Peadar interjected. 'He can switch workmen around all he likes once he meets his commitments to us, because he knows he's not getting another red cent until I can see my face shining in the floor tiles.'

Peadar replaced the receiver, making a deliberate show of switching the phone off.

'Sorry about that,' he apologised.

'No, it's reassuring,' Alison replied. 'Once I'm sure McCann is still in Dublin I know he can't pop his head out of the petrol tank if we stop to fill it up somewhere along the way.'

Peadar smiled, knowing her views on the vice-principal. She used to tease him in bed by inventing blind dates for McCann, her favourite being to pair him off with Mother Teresa.

The Enid Blyton tape had run out. Alison turned it over.

Pip, Fatty and Daisy continued outwitting the fat policeman, Mr Goon, on side two. Danny was fascinated though he had heard it a dozen times before. Shane was happy beside him, playing some game with Paddington Bear. And Sheila . . . Sheila was simply happy, like it was a gift she'd been born with. Sheila, with the same jet-black hair as herself, whom they very nearly didn't have. They had even seen a doctor about Peadar having the operation before finally deciding to go once again. Three boys would have been too much, but Alison had been certain from the moment Sheila was conceived that there was a girl inside her. Never mind that she had felt the same about Shane for nine months and told anyone who asked her. This time she'd known in her bones and kept the secret to herself.

She turned to smile at her daughter as Peadar edged in and out, trying to glimpse the winding road ahead where a gap was developing between the jeep and horsebox and the cars in front. Sheila smiled back, almost conspiratorially. Sheila who never lost her temper, even when a note arrived before the start of the Easter holidays ten days ago stating that Jean O'Connor in her class had meningitis and Alison had driven her daughter crazy, shining lights in her eyes and searching for a rash at every hour of the night. Sheila who would be her companion when the boys and Peadar were off at football games. Boys leave home and leave their mothers, but girls never quite do. They row and argue in their teens, worrying their mothers senseless, but in the end gradually become friends and confidantes in a way that no son could ever be. That's what she had missed, with her own mother dying of cancer when Alison was twenty-two. The pendulum had never swung back. There was so much they could have talked about now, so many questions Alison would love to ask. She reached one finger out and Sheila's hot hand wrapped itself around it, twiddling with the eternity ring she loved to turn in the light.

'Are we there yet, Mama?' she asked.

Alison shook her head as Peadar indicated and pulled out. At once she knew something was wrong by the intake of Peadar's breath. Alison looked around. He was on the wrong side of the road, just where the white line started to break up. A blue van was coming towards them, but there would be time for Peadar to pull in again in front of the jeep pulling the horsebox. The problem was the black BMW with lights flashing behind them. She had noticed the bearded driver's impatience earlier on and sensed how his constant swaying made Peadar nervous. Now the driver was trying to simultaneously overtake them and the jeep. The man was beeping furiously, screaming at Peadar through the glass like it was his fault. Peadar veered in front of the jeep, putting his foot down to try and create enough space before the BMW swerved into the side of them. The blue van flashed past. Alison screamed, waiting for the crash but somehow the BMW had managed to squeeze in behind them, mainly because the jeep braked hard, sending the horsebox swaying about on the road.

The BMW's lights were only inches from their back bumper, feet away from her children. Peadar was rattled, shouting at Alison for screaming, cursing the lunatic behind them. The BMW pulled out again without indicating and sped into the distance. Alison could see two teenage girls looking back at them vacantly through the rear window.

Peadar said something and she snapped back. Then they both went quiet, anxious not to frighten the children more. She raised the volume on the tape, sat back and stared ahead. Peadar went slower than usual, even though the road was clear. Cars overtook them, flashing back at twenty and thirty miles above the speed limit. He looked across after five minutes and took her hand in his free one.

'It wasn't my fault,' he said quietly. 'I'd never take chances with you all in the car. It was that lunatic.'

She squeezed his hand and said nothing. What would it matter whose fault it was if they were all dead on the roadside? She wished they were in the hotel already, the children splashing about in the pool and her outside in the Canadian hot tub. The tape ended. Three voices called out different requests, but she ignored them, not even looking for music on the radio. She needed silence to get her wits back. She wanted to close her eyes as she always did at some stage of this journey and become a child again, counting off the miles in the clank of wheels as the train brought her mother and father and herself on that one magical holiday to Fitzgerald's.

---

They didn't stop again on the way down and the children were quiet, leaving her to her memories. Arklow was now by-passed and Enniscorthy wasn't too slow. As Peadar picked up speed along the banks of the Slaney with the asylum perched on the cliffs above them, she searched for the Ginger-bread Man tape. There was something about the snatches of classical background music and the narrator's voice saying 'at the blip turn the page' that conjured up for her the pent-up expectation of every journey they had taken on this road. She could remember playing it for Danny when Shane was a baby and then for Shane when Sheila was teething beside him in the car. Even at home when she put it on and closed her eyes she could see this stretch of road and feel the spring sunshine through the windscreen as the car sped along these last few miles.

The boys protested at the choice of tape but she told them that it was Sheila's turn to hear something.

'Just twenty miles,' Peadar told Danny, 'and we're there. No more towns or anything, just open road.'

Wexford town was long by-passed, taking the Rosslare traffic away from those cramped medieval streets she had first glimpsed as the train trundled slowly over wooden quayside sleepers the summer she was twelve. Holding a bottle of Guinness by the neck, her father had pulled down the carriage window and stared out, lost in memories of which she had no part.

Weeks before, when the notion of a special holiday to mark his silver wedding anniversary arose, her father had been adamant about doing it in style by taking his wife and young daughter down to Fitzgerald's. It was the first time she had ever heard of the hotel, but he began describing it as like a palace. His own father had taken him there by train from Waterford for lunch when he made his Confirmation in the 1930s, an extravagant day trip they had spent years talking about. And the summer after he left school at fourteen he had got a kitchen job there, living in, and bathing on the private beach every evening.

Standing at the train window, he had seemed to change

before her eyes. Hidden fragments of his life tumbled out that she strove to piece together. This was the first occasion when she properly understood that parents had previous lives and secrets. Listening to him had reminded her of a boy with his nose pressed against a shop window. Always on the outside, describing the clothes guests wore to dinner back then, the size of the dining room, the musicians who played. All as glimpsed from a kitchen sink, between the swish of a swing door opening and closing as waiters came and went. Now he had decided to return with his wife and daughter in his own private triumph.

Alison could remember the tiny station at Rosslare and the steep hump-backed bridge where the sea suddenly glistened into sight. They had walked the few hundred yards to the hotel, him in front with two heavy suitcases, she and her mother straggling slightly behind. She had felt a nervousness for her father. He seemed out of his depth, striding forward with a frighteningly boyish eagerness. Even at twelve she sensed he was going to be disappointed by the fact that nobody knew him, no one recalled his hands scrubbing pots in scalding water, nobody would understand the momentous nature of his return.

Yet all this she only fully understood years later, when Danny was two and Alison spent a week in Waterford after her father's funeral, sorting out clothes and personal effects, filling in the gaps of his life through them. He had known poverty in Waterford as a boy and later on in London. Yet he always took whatever work would provide a home for his wife and his two London-born sons. The younger boy was ten before he returned to Waterford to work in the glass factory and the afterthought or mistake occurred that became her. That was a question you didn't ask your parents back then, even if in adolescence the doubt had tortured her.

Either way all she knew was love, unburdened by the expectations that Peadar seemed to carry from his earliest years. She still remembered hearing her father rise an hour before the rest of them, the bolt being drawn back and his boots on the path disturbing her childhood sleep as he set off for the early shift. Surely he was sick sometimes but she never recalled it. He had simply got on with what had to be done for his children. But that trip to Fitzgerald's had been for him alone. It was the moment when he could rest among the soft arm-chairs and know that his life's main work was done, with one son married, a second finishing his apprenticeship and his only daughter due to be the first member of his family to ever complete secondary school.

She, meanwhile, had been preoccupied with discovering the swimming pool, the crazy golf, the private beach and the food. She had known her first kiss at Fitzgerald's, sitting on a rock at twilight near the steps up from the beach. Three days of intense expectation with a thirteen-year-old boy from Newry had built up to that moment. The feel of his tongue for the eternity of a second before she turned and ran off, back up the steps into the safety of childhood. How could you explain time to a child? Ten or twenty years that suddenly pass? It was more than a quarter of a century since her first solitary kiss at Fitzgerald's. How many lifetimes ago did that moment seem? A foreboding crept over her in the car, a melancholic hangover from last night's dream. What if this was all the future held, a succession of cars carrying her ever-ageing body down to this hotel? Forty soon, then fifty, sixty. She closed her eyes, feeling the car speed forward, unstoppable, on a journey she had no control over.

She opened them again to glance back at her children's excited faces. They had passed the last roundabout for Wexford town and the N25 for Waterford. These were the final miles, past the turnoff for Kilmore Quay and through Killinick in the wink of an eye. Sheila silently mouthed the words 'How much longer?' and suddenly Alison felt like a child herself again. She strained to glimpse the sign for the turn left, which took them down the wide country road with a dozen signs on every bend for hotels and guesthouses and always, the fourth one down, for Fitzgerald's.

They were here now, a turn left at a garage, a sharp right again and the railway bridge was before them. Soon the first glimpse of the sea. The children craned their necks forward. But it was different for them, not like the solitary time she had come all those years ago. They expected this as a right, year after year, their break at Fitzgerald's, remarkable and yet routine. They were excited, yet she wanted their excitement to be more. She half resented the fact they were not shouting with joy. She wanted brass bands, she didn't know what she wanted. She wanted to look out and see her father straining under his suitcases. She wanted to call, 'We're here by right now, Dad, year after year.' She wanted to feel twelve again. She wanted to cry, remembering how she had honestly expected never to see this hotel again except as a woman riddled with cancer.

Peadar turned left and suddenly it was there, on the right, rising up in cream and blue, with tennis courts visible and palm trees in the garden. Every year something changed, every year something new, but still always it was Fitzgerald's.

The car park on the left was crammed with sleek cars, with one battered old van incongruously among them. Peadar drove in through the cream pillars and found a spot near the grass. He flung his door open, his shoulders stiff from driving, and opened the back door for Danny to jump up into his arms. He threw his son into the air and caught him as Danny raised his fist like he'd scored a goal.

'Fitzgerald's,' Danny said. 'We're here, Daddy, we're here!'

Shane and Sheila clambered out, running to the wall to peer across at it. Their faces were mesmerised. Peadar walked around the car to put his arm around her, then looked down.

'Hey,' he asked quietly, 'why are you crying?'

She looked at him. She remembered her mother dying, her father lost and left behind. She remembered herself as an overlooked child in this hotel, the future she had imagined. She remembered how close that BMW had come to killing them, the coldness of Dr O'Gorman's hand on her breast. Alison put her arms around him.

'You big fool,' she said. 'I'm crying because I'm happy.'

⁓

The welcoming sherry reception was in the foyer at seven o'clock. In the early years Peadar and herself had laughed at it and never attended, but now it seemed an integral part of their holiday. By six-thirty the major unpacking was done and strolling down to the foyer forced her to relax. The boys were asking about it from the time they had taken their first swim at half-four. To them 'reception' had the same ring as 'party' and a party was still a party even if it only consisted of adults in suits chatting away on the striped sofas.

She knew they would get bored of it within minutes. Once they had clung to her side as Sheila did now, with the colouring book and crayons she would soon tire of and demand to be snuggled up instead on Alison's knee. The boys waited only to get glasses of orange juice from the bow-tied waiters at the white table beside the dining room windows. Danny drained his glass and called to Shane. Like a shadow, his younger brother followed him down the corridor, ready to turn the slightest occurrence into an adventure.

Alison was happy to let them go, once she could keep an eye on the main doorway. Danny had finally reached an age to explore by himself and she knew how he loved to delve into every corner and alcove of the hotel. There were so many rooms he would have to peek into: the card room that was always empty; the smoking room with its blazing log fire even on summer nights; the TV room where Geraldine and Aoife, the children's activities co-ordinators, were already screening the first evening's video. The boys would settle down to watch it shortly, but Danny still insisted on either Peadar or her sitting in an armchair in the corridor. For all his new found toughness, ghosts and dinosaurs frightened him and they would have to be within reach if the film grew too scary.

The babysitter was due at eight. Alison hoped it wouldn't be one of those teenage girls it was impossible to get a word from. The usual bedtime arguments were still an hour away. For now Sheila was happy colouring and Peadar had fallen into reluctant conversation at the table where the waiters were pouring more sherry. She could tell by the way he held the sherry glasses, poised to flee back to her. The tall man in the suit beside him laughed at what Peadar obviously hoped was a closing remark.

'Yes, yes,' she heard the man's booming voice agree. 'It's great to forget the pressures of work and relax. So tell me, what do *you* do?'

Peadar caught her glance and discreetly threw his eyes to heaven. She knew he was too polite to disentangle himself from the conversation and also that, like a mother with a first child, he would soon begin to talk about the school extension. She didn't mind. She was enjoying these rare moments alone. Two elderly couples on the sofas beside her were making friends. A waitress bent to offer her a tray of hors d'oeuvres. She finished her first sherry and looked around. Other hotels might have leisure centres and chefs that were equally good, but she had never seen anywhere to match Fitzgerald's paintings. And they weren't just the safe landscapes you saw elsewhere. Here paintings accosted you; some stunning, many unfathomable but every one challenging. She had grown to know the names by now: Le Broquy, Crozier, Nora McGuinness, Patrick Collins and fantastical childhood landscapes by Martin Gale that the boys loved to stare at.

Sheila pulled at her sleeve for attention, holding up a page from her colouring book streaked almost entirely with red crayon. Alison praised it and found her another page to colour. She looked up and a face caught her attention, although she wasn't sure why. It had a disconcerting familiarity, yet the man it belonged to looked somehow out of place. He leaned down, replying to some remark from a couple in their fifties seated beside the piano player.

She recognised them as the Bennetts. They were childless, Scottish and superb dancers. They came for five nights at Easter and another week in October and entered every competition. Each Thursday night at prizegiving they walked across the dance floor to receive Fitzgerald's mugs and plates for table tennis, indoor bowls and crazy golf. She wondered what they did with their endless supply of crockery and liked to imagine Mrs Bennett having tantrums, smashing things, while the petite Mr Bennett screamed, 'No, dear, please, not the table quiz mug!'

Mrs Bennett looked up and waved in recognition. Alison smiled back as both Mr Bennett and the man glanced in her direction. The man's gaze perturbed her. There was something not right about him, like a photo-fit that didn't match. His skin seemed younger than his eyes. She couldn't explain why this bothered her. There were so many faces you saw here year after year. Nobody could expect to remember them all. She looked away, feigning great interest in Sheila's colouring, yet aware that the man was leaving the Bennetts and walking towards her. He even seemed to slow down as she kept her head buried over her daughter's colouring book, then he strolled on, past Mr Diekhoff and his son, to wherever he had parked his own wife.

Mr Diekhoff had been coming here from Cologne for twenty-five years, ever since his son, Heinrich, was four. Alison watched the Down's Syndrome boy sit quietly beside his widowed father. Strictly speaking he wasn't a boy, but she couldn't think of him as approaching thirty, no more than she could bear to imagine his life if he outlived his father. Heinrich's presence here – politely asking women he knew for one dance and perpetually winning the crazy golf competition – was another talisman of her holiday. It was fifteen years since his mother had died, but his father resolutely continued this annual trip to the hotel he had discovered as a young hitchhiker. Alison knew he came for Heinrich's sake more than his own – although he had his friends among the regulars here. He sensed her glance at him and smiled in greeting. She felt the weight of responsibility in his eyes as Heinrich waved to her cheerfully.

Peadar finally returned with the sherries, having extracted himself from the man's company. 'What a bore,' he said. 'An RTE producer. You know the type who stop strangers on the street when they can't find anyone else to argue with.'

She looked around, meaning to ask Peadar if he recognised the stranger, when somebody else caught her attention.

'The bastard,' she hissed, making Peadar look at her in surprise. She nodded towards a sofa near the reception desk where a bearded man was smoking and enjoying a whiskey while his teenage daughters sulked over the orange juices before them.

'Do we know him?' Peadar asked.

'He's the bastard in the BMW who nearly got us killed. Do you not remember the pusses on those two girls gawking out the window?'

The bearded man stared directly back and raised his glass as if in a toast, although Alison couldn't be sure if he recognised them. She had already risen when Peadar grabbed her arm.

'Where're you going?'

34

'To throw my sherry over the smug bastard.'

'Ah, Jaysus, please don't,' Peadar cajoled. 'It will take me half an hour to get you another one if that RTE arsehole spots me going back up to the table.'

'I'm serious.'

The man seemed to be watching, amused and impervious to what was going on. His daughters had even forgotten to look bored.

'For God's sake, Alison, what's the point? Don't spoil our holiday. You know you're like a bag of cats on the first night here anyway.'

Danny and Shane appeared in the foyer, checking they were still there. Sheila wanted Alison to praise her colouring. Alison sat back angrily, but Peadar was right. He was always bloody right, especially when it came to her losing her temper. And she did find it hard to relax on the first night here, from a cocktail of memory and guilt.

Every year they came here the menu changed but some traditional Fitzgerald recipes remained the same. She remembered her parents uneasily stirring the green nettle and cognac soup that was still served here. And how she herself had half expected to be stung as she raised the soup spoon to her lips. Nettle soup to them was something from the famine, the poorest of the poor boiling weeds for nourishment. They couldn't have been more shocked if the main course had consisted of the old recipe of potatoes mashed with blood from a cut made in a cow's leg. As it was, they had been taken aback by the litany of penitent fish dishes even though it wasn't a Friday.

Her parents had been perpetually ill at ease on that holiday, her mother making the beds each morning and frantically tidying up before the cleaners came in. They had sat in armchairs in the Slaney Room, talking mainly to the staff and just watching other guests pass by. She had only ever seen them this uncomfortable again whenever they were forced to meet Peadar's parents. They had not fitted in here and neither had she. The other children tolerated her mainly for her novelty value, making her repeat phrases in her Waterford accent. Only the Newry boy had treated her differently, thrown together by them being the only two children not from Dublin.

It perturbed her every time she returned, just how well she fitted in here now, how indistinguishable her children were from the others running in and out of the television room. The same Dublin accents, with hardly a trace of her Waterford or Peadar's Galway brogue – not that she herself had much of an accent left. Her parents would be proud. Yet this never stopped her from imagining them, perched on a sofa in this foyer, speaking in whispers and not recognising the daughter who had left them behind in trying to meet the expectations of her in-laws.

It was best to get the children ready before the babysitter came. She rose and walked towards the boys, praising her self-control in ignoring the bearded man when he spoke to her.

'You need to trade in those wheels of yours,' he joked, like the incident had been amusing. 'Get something with a bit more vroom in it.'

She stared at him.

'Maybe that's what you need yourself.' He looked puzzled, his daughters moronically staring through her like she wasn't there. Her accent thickened, reverting back to girlhood. 'I mean these things are about compensation, aren't they?'

'I don't see how compensation enters into it,' he said, defensive now, watchful of his wallet. 'There was no accident, nobody hurt, nothing.'

'I don't mean that type of compensation.' She was aware of Peadar anxiously at her shoulder. 'I mean the other kind, the need to make up for things. Or as we say in Waterford, the bigger the horsepower the smaller the prick behind the wheel.'

She walked on, aware of the silence behind her, of the girls staring and of Peadar at her shoulder. They got around the corner before Peadar managed to speak.

'His face,' he said. 'You should have seen the gobshite's face.' Both started laughing, unable to stop, collapsing onto the nearest sofa, while the boys hovered, convinced their parents were cracking up. Danny's eight-year-old face was such a picture of mortified respectability that he could have passed for Peadar's father.

'Stop it,' he hissed, 'you're embarrassing me.'

Alison pulled him onto her lap, tickling him as he struggled and the others jumped up in a tangle of limbs. Now she felt truly on holidays.

———— ❧ ————

Throughout dinner she knew they were going to make love that night. She kicked off her shoes and played footsie with Peadar, even when Jack Fitzgerald himself stopped to welcome them back. She could feel Peadar's shoe gently brush her calf, then explore upwards between her bare knees as the owner moved off and the waitress took their order for dessert. During the two days of packing she usually just pecked at snacks, too flustered to feel hungry. This always made their first meal all the more special.

There was never music in the Slaney Room on Sunday nights. Older couples gathered around the piano instead in the French Bar at the far end of the building. Alison and Peadar enjoyed their coffees in the foyer near the open fire. The porter got them drinks and Peadar allowed himself his usual single cigar. The heat from the logs scorched Alison's legs. Yet she loved the smell of wood-smoke. She would happily have gone back to the room then but they waited a little longer to make it worth the babysitter's while. They nestled like lovers, her head against his chest, nursing their second drinks until sufficient time had elapsed.

The boys were asleep in single beds on either side of the double one, with Sheila snuggled down in a third bed near the French doors that opened out onto gardens overlooking the sea. Peadar had his hands under the waistband of her skirt while she was still closing the door on the babysitter. She turned and he picked her up, her legs straddling his waist as he carried her towards the bed. He collapsed on top of her, each shushing the other while simultaneously trying not to laugh. He undid the top of her outfit, his hands gripping her silk slip as if about to tear it off, while her eyes warned him against trying any such thing. He worked it upwards, his hands managing to undo her bra while she kissed him and tugged at his zip.

She wasn't sure if their noise caused Danny to shift, his

legs kicking the blankets off. But pure instinct made her slide out from under Peadar and go to fix the blankets. Peadar raised a hand to silently stop her, yet even as she touched Danny she knew she was crazy not to leave the boy alone. When would she learn to stop meddling until it was necessary to do so? She tucked in the blankets then turned back to Peadar but the mood was already broken. He looked past her to where Danny stirred again. He was not a child you could disturb in his sleep. He was half awake now and half dreaming, sitting up to call for her in distress and yet not realising she was already there. Alison settled him down once more but knew it was no use.

'Take him out, quickly,' Peadar hissed, but she hesitated, hoping against hope the boy would settle back asleep. Danny sat up and cried, making the first retching noise in his throat. His eyes were open but she knew that everything seemed like a bad dream for him. Peadar grabbed him and ran, getting his head over the toilet before the vomit came. Danny cried as he retched again, with his whole dinner coming up.

Alison watched from the bathroom door, cursing herself and knowing Peadar was silently cursing her too. Danny's pyjamas were untouched. There were just a few specks on the tiles and on Peadar's shoes. Peadar carried him back to bed and tucked him in. The child would sleep peacefully now till morning.

Her clothes were disarrayed, but she knew her semi-nakedness wasn't arousing any more. It was the mundane nudity of child raising. Her nipples looked flat and worn, but Peadar wasn't even gazing at her.

'I might get a last drink,' he whispered, as though anxious

to extricate himself. 'You read if you like, I'll only be a few minutes.'

She wanted to stop him, to suggest they try again, but it was too late. She let him go, undressed and turned the lights out. It was wrong to think that Peadar was punishing her. It just wasn't like ten years ago, when he seemed to develop a permanent erection whenever they were alone. Kids changed you and three kids wore you out. You saw your partner in situations that modesty would once never have allowed. Neither of them had been able for a third child if they were honest – no more than her own parents had been. Let Peadar enjoy his drink, let his tension subside. She found she was still damp. Her fingers touched the spot idly, wondering why his tongue always had such difficulty in locating it.

A noise outside froze her hand. A footstep on gravel beyond the French doors. For a second she thought that maybe it was Peadar, crazily planning to surprise her, to rekindle the spontaneity which had once marked their lovemaking. But he would know the door was locked. It had to be a burglar. But the kids had been racing in and out all afternoon. Was she sure she had remembered to lock the French doors? She wished Peadar was here. She waited for the click of a hand to test the handle but there was just silence as if the footsteps had moved on or she had imagined the whole affair.

She lay curled in the dark. I gave up my happiness to make another person happy, she found herself thinking, to make my family happy. I am who I've become because this is who they need me to be. When I got the all-clear I wasn't even happy for myself. It was them I was thinking of. I couldn't die because other people needed me. But what do I need?

The image returned from last night, a woman swaying under water, her lifeless hands against the glass, waiting to be chanced upon by some diver.

Her body felt old and stale. Her hand was motionless between her thighs. The rich food lay heavily on her stomach while her children's breathing filled the room. She was on holidays, the treat she had so looked forward to. So why did she feel alone, like she had woken to find she was leading another person's life inside somebody else's skin?

# MONDAY

Sheila woke first. Alison could tell by the springs of the small bed and knew that her daughter was content to lie there, self-contained, savouring the wonder of waking in a hotel bedroom. Shane would sleep on, even feigning sleep for a time after he woke, but Danny would be out of bed once his eyes opened. Alison lay on her side, watching her elder son's sleeping face, knowing that his eyelids would flicker automatically open at half past seven. Every morning the same so that she had stopped using an alarm clock.

She couldn't tell if Peadar was awake or asleep. It had been late when he returned from the bar and she hadn't turned over, forcing him to make the first move, if any. She knew that he had lain awake for a long time, with inches of sheet separating their skin. She turned towards him now. His breath was nasally and in a few years' time he would snore. He looked older in the dawn light, worn out, although she knew that once he woke he would summon the energy to sparkle and make the children laugh. He was a morning person. Perhaps that was one of the contrasts which made their marriage work.

She spooned herself into his back and put an arm around him, her fingers luxuriating along his furry chest, then moving mischievously down to the untidy tangle of hair spilling out from his Y-fronts. He stirred, sleepily, as her fingers lightly brushed against the unsummoned stiffness he sometimes woke with.

'I've told you, McCann,' he murmured, 'my wife is getting suspicious.'

It was an established joke between them. 'Very suspicious,' she whispered back, gently taking his earlobe between her teeth. Peadar turned towards her and the creak of their bed woke Danny who padded across to snuggle sleepily against her back, his eyes not even fully open. Peadar rolled over to disguise his stiffness as Danny leaned across to hug his father. All three lay in silence, then Peadar turned more fully onto his stomach as Sheila joined them on his side of the bed. Alison smiled, wondering what cold unerotic thoughts he was filtering through his head.

'The plunge pool,' she muttered to him.

'What?'

'Think of diving into the ice-cold plunge pool.'

Peadar shivered loudly. 'I was thinking of McCann with Mother Teresa,' he replied and stared across at Shane still feigning sleep and clutching his Paddington Bear.

'I've an idea,' he said. 'Let's all eat Paddington for breakfast.'

'You will not.' Shane uncoiled himself and landed with one spring on their bed. Peadar laughed and soon had the children laughing too, as he invented songs, with no trace of disappointment in his voice at the sexual tension which, just a few moments before, seemed about to spill over between them.

Alison was relieved some years back when Peadar stopped attempting to explain the rules of the Fitzgerald's golfing scramble competition to her. It combined the complexity of Einstein's theory of relativity with a propensity for appalling dress sense on the part of more serious disciples. For lesser mortals like Peadar it apparently consisted of three strangers teeing off, almost everybody picking their ball up again, everyone blaming the prevailing weather conditions or their hangovers and promising to buy each other a drink in the hotel bar that night.

However, she knew it kept Peadar happy for a few hours on the Monday morning, after which he was generally content to put his golf clubs away for the remainder of the holiday. The biggest cheer at the prizegiving every Thursday night was for the golfing competition, with scores calculated by a formula, based on points from individual rounds and a percentage of points from the scramble, which seemed better applied to nuclear physics. Alison could spot the men and women who spent whole days trying to better their scores, and evenings huddled at the bar working out minute calculations.

Every year Peadar simply put his name down to make up the numbers for some old couple's scramble team and steered clear of everything else. Alison told him she didn't mind if he entered the competition properly by playing a full solo round now that the children were older. But she knew how a sense of duty held him back from abandoning her for so long. His scramble partners this year, the Irwins, came from Northern Ireland. They hailed him at breakfast time, with Peadar jokingly saluting Mr Irwin as 'captain' and arranging to meet them on the first tee at eleven o'clock.

It was only after Peadar had left and she brought the children for their morning swim, that she realised Danny was now too big to be taken into the ladies' changing room. She had to ask an attendant to stay in the gents' locker room with him, and even then she was uneasy, not recognising him from any previous year.

She got Sheila and Shane changed quickly and brought them out to where Danny waited impatiently at the poolside. The attendant smiled and walked away to fix the pile of towels, making Alison feel guilty for harbouring suspicions about him.

There were two full-size pools, a kiddies' one sloping to a depth of five feet and an eight-foot adult one nearly always empty. The sauna and steam rooms were hidden behind statues up steps beside the adult pool, with a plunge pool between them. Out on the terrace, once you braved the sea breeze and occasional rain, was an outdoor Canadian hot tub whose powerful jets of water made the indoor jacuzzi almost tepid by comparison.

Alison knew she would have to give these pleasures a miss this morning to keep an eye on the children. The boys dived straight into the kiddies' pool. Sheila ran to the steps and waded in. Alison followed slowly, shivering and warning them to let her lower her body into the cold water in her own time. Either her bathing costume had shrunk or else her bottom was getting bigger. She needed to discreetly adjust it under the water. The kiddies' pool was packed. She looked around, wondering if the boys would make friends this year and might Sheila be left out of things.

Parents took turns minding children while their partners lazed in the steam room or raced outdoors in their bare feet to chance the Canadian hot tub. Danny was a natural swimmer, although Shane stubbornly insisted on wearing one armband. Alison mainly played with Sheila, letting the boys invent chasing games of their own. Somebody switched the fountain on and a thin sheet of water spilled down as children splashed excitedly underneath it. She saw the man who had spoken to the Bennetts last night, just for a second among hordes of parents and children at the pool edge. Then Danny popped up before her, splashing water and looking for a chase. She swam after him in mock rage while Shane joined the pursuit and, from the corner of her eye, Alison noticed Sheila playing with a girl her own age. A powerful water jet burst into life, spraying out a current in the far corner of the pool. She caught Danny who wriggled free and threw himself headlong into the turbulent spray.

Alison turned as Shane followed his brother, knowing the jet would keep the boys busy. That man was watching her again, this time from the Jacuzzi overlooking the children's pool. He had obviously left his own brood to be attended by his wife. Instinctively she knew he had been watching for a long time, but he didn't look away, even when she stared back. Instead he nodded slightly. Maybe their families had shared a holiday here before but that didn't give him the right to blatantly eyeball her. She thought about how her bathing costume had shrunk and wondered had he seen her enter the pool. Sheila swam towards her. Alison made a great fuss of picking her daughter up, annoyed at him and furious at herself for feeling vaguely flattered. But it was a while since any man had gazed at her like that.

When Alison allowed herself to gaze back after five

minutes the man had left the Jacuzzi. She glanced around the pool, wondered which mother was his wife and whether she knew that her husband stared at strangers.

Someone was calling her name. She recognised the wild brood of kids jumping into the water before she saw Joan, a woman from Dundalk who had shared this same week as them for the last three years. Alison smiled, recalling Joan's raucous laugh and how she loved to stay up half the night, gathering other women around her to tell blue jokes.

If they lived near each other in Dublin, then Alison suspected that Joan was the sort of woman she would spend her life avoiding. But here on holidays it was good to have a laugh, without knowing that everything you said would be spun out as exaggerated gossip in the local park. Alison's two sisters-in-law in Waterford had the same small-town look, getting drunk together at Joe Dolan concerts one night, falling out with each other the next. But at least they were there for one another, even though increasingly distant towards Alison every time she went back to Waterford.

Joan dived in, shivering with the sudden cold. She swam towards Alison, happily complaining in her usual torrent of words: 'Is your Peadar beating the bushes on the golf course for lost balls like my Joey? I keep telling him, "Joey, you can't piss in a straight line never mind hit a golf ball." Joey's version of course management is not falling into a lake and drowning himself.'

Joan aimed a palmful of water at her eldest son who threatened to swim too near.

'Would you look at Jason there and him so sick last night we had to eat in our room. I saw Peadar at the bar when I finally got down but you were tucked away out of sight. He must have shagged you out, you know these schoolmasters and their big sticks. Here, off you go and have a sauna while I'll keep an eye on your three.'

Alison went to protest but Joan raised a mock fist.

'Away with you.' She turned towards Danny who had swum over, recognising her and knowing a chase was on the cards. 'Look at the size of you, Danny! They must be stretching you each night to make sure you make the right height for the cops. Come here till I squash you back to your proper size!'

Alison clambered out, listening to his mock screams and grateful for a few moments' peace. Neither Shane nor Sheila noticed her slip away. She stood over the adult pool, knowing the water there was even colder. That man still hadn't relieved his wife of her childminding duties. Alison saw him emerge from the sauna and stand beside the plunge pool. She never got down into it herself, despite Peadar's protestations that a sauna was useless without icy water afterwards to close over the pores. But even Peadar himself always climbed down gingerly, shivering as she teased him. Alison watched the man, with his back to her, as he looked into the freezing water, then suddenly let his body fall with a splash. She shuddered, and panicked when there seemed no sign of his head reappearing. The plunge pool was seven foot deep, with a ladder going only half way down.

She looked around but nobody else was paying any attention. She had taken a step towards the plunge pool when his head resurfaced, spraying out drops of water as he shook his hair like a drenched dog. He turned, catching sight of her and nodded again. Alison found herself looking away as if caught spying. She dived into the adult pool, shivering but then enjoying its childfree waters. She swam towards the deep end, as far as possible from his eyes. She couldn't be sure if her sense of still being watched was instinct or paranoia.

Alison swam lengths until her arms ached, then discreetly checked that the children weren't missing her. A young mother held a crying baby in the crowded pool, glaring angrily towards the sauna, obviously waiting for her overdue husband. Alison smiled, imagining the reception that awaited him. Joan spied her and waved her away again. She checked the clock, allowing herself ten minutes before getting the kids changed for lunch.

The teenage Dublin girls had just arrived in bikinis and dived in unison into the adult pool. They climbed out again to repeat the exercise, in case any man present had missed it. Their father was heading into the sauna with the RTE executive who had cornered Peadar last night. She imagined them ladling more water onto the hot coals, anxious to outdo each other in the macho stakes as they discussed horsepower, horse-trading and horse shit.

She chose the steam room instead which was empty or at first appeared to be. She stretched out on the upper tier of hot tiles, adjusting her bathing costume, and stared up at the slow drip-drip of water converging and falling from the corners of tiles in the curved roof. It took several moments for her eyes to adjust to the steam and for the blurred outline of a man sitting against the far wall to register. She knew without being able to distinguish any features that it was him. Alison cursed herself for picking the steam room, then became angry. She had often shared this space with men before without it costing her a thought. If he was a voyeur that was his problem not hers. Besides he couldn't get more steamed up than he was already. Alison lay back, closed her eyes and decided to ignore him.

'They say five minutes in here earns you five years off purgatory.' His voice broke the silence, as if he knew she had only now become aware of him. Alison made a non-committal noise, hoping to discourage him. But he laughed instead, wryly and familiarly. 'We could have used some of this heat, stuck out at night in that mobile library in Skerries.'

Alison lay perfectly still. Mentally she checked her bathing costume, the state of her hair, a half dozen inconsequential things as she tried to place his voice. She felt naked, stripped of her anonymity. It was twenty years since she had briefly worked in the mobile libraries. She opened her eyes and tried to peer across through the steam.

'Do I know you?' she asked.

'A different time, Ali, a different world.'

How long was it since anyone called her Ali? The nickname had only been used by a handful of people. It was a brief benchmark of freedom at eighteen when she got her first job away from Waterford. The mobile libraries were a stopgap until she started training as a nurse the following April. Everyone working there had a pet name that summer. The three lads sharing the top table all called themselves Harold. 'Is Harold in yet, Harold?' 'No, I haven't seen him, Harold.' Betty was known as Sheila because she wanted to emigrate to Australia. Sharon was called Lucy because she phoned in sick to smoke dope in her bedsit and watch reruns of *Here's Lucy* – a programme she swore she hated but not as much as she hated work. The nickname Ali had suited Alison back then, the bright sparkle of it as she floated like a butterfly through late-night library parties in bedsits.

In Dublin, being called Ali made her feel different from the child she became again when she took the train home each weekend. That's what nicknames did, made you part of something special. It was why Peadar renamed her Alison within weeks of them meeting that summer, like her real name had turned full circle to become an intimate term of endearment between them. But she felt flustered in the steam room now and knew the man could sense it, because his voice changed, growing almost apologetic.

'I hope I didn't startle you,' he said. 'I saw you last night and couldn't believe my eyes. I knew you hadn't a clue who I was. You mightn't remember me anyway. But, of course, the beard doesn't help, or the absence of it. You used to joke that at twenty I looked forty with it and at forty I'd shave it off and look twenty again.'

'Chris?'

Good Christ, she thought, not Chris Conway here, all of a slap, in the steam room at Fitzgerald's. Chris had never needed a nickname. A manic explosion of jokes and gestures, he always stood out simply as Chris.

'You've barely changed, Ali. You must have a portrait of yourself growing old in your attic.'

She laughed, flattered and embarrassed. The beard. That's what had perturbed her about the face yesterday. Chris Conway. A dozen memories jostled together. Laughing as he persuaded her to take a piggyback off him all the way to the bank to cash her first pay cheque. The Friday afternoon himself and a driver went to do a stop in Tallaght and the mobile van was spotted on Sunday morning, still not returned from a remote pub car park up the Wicklow Mountains. His tricks to torment and thwart the old librarian who liked to bully female trainees. But Chris was right, the memories came from a different world. It was ten years since Peadar last mentioned him, something about the book trade. Alison didn't know what to say, so she tried a joke.

'You're in trouble.'

'Sorry?' he replied.

'Your wife . . .'

'Yes.'

'You can expect a frosty reception. I mean you're hardly a new man, are you, leaving her with the kids all this time?'

The door opened and Mr BMW came in. He sat on the tier below her, grunting contentedly like a bloated Roman emperor. A drop of water hit her nose and ran slowly down onto her lips. She felt Chris wanted to say something but was inhibited by the man's presence. That would be just like Chris, she thought. The silence seemed so awkward that for a moment she wondered if she'd made a mistake.

'You *are* married?' she asked.

'I married all right.'

'Kids?'

'Two girls,' Chris replied. 'I saw your kids in the pool. They're lovely, the wee one especially.'

'Another father of girls,' Mr BMW cut in, as though he owned the conversation. 'Sweet suffering Jesus, when you are the father of daughters you pray.'

Chris didn't reply. He picked up the drenched towel he'd been using as a pillow and pushed the door open.

'I hope she doesn't lynch you,' Alison teased but Chris never looked back. Ignoring her, Mr BMW stretched out on the tiles below so that Alison would have to step over him to exit. Above the hissing steam she heard the splash of a body entering the plunge pool. For some reason she found herself counting the seconds until another splash told her that Chris's head had emerged again.

It was time to return to her own kids but she waited to let Chris get ahead of her. A sign on the wall prohibited children and the use of oils in the steam room. It didn't mention stilettos, she thought, glancing at the obese belly on display below, as if waiting for slaves to carry its owner off to the vomitorium. She decided Mr BMW would probably enjoy that too much. Alison stepped carefully around him and pushed open the door, glad to escape from the heat. The water in the plunge pool still rippled after Chris. She decided that if her pores wanted to close badly enough they could do so by themselves.

The mother who had been glaring towards the sauna now swam alone in the adult pool. She was about thirty-three, Alison reckoned, though she could even be younger. A bathing hat could not contain her long fair hair. As she reached the far wall and kicked over to swim on her back, Alison found herself watching, comparing their features and figures, noticing how the woman's willowy arms moved without effort through the water. It was ridiculous to feel a stab of jealousy. There was no way Alison would ever have become Chris's wife. But she wanted to know if Chris loved this woman, not in the understated way most men love their wives, but like he had once loved her. Back when she was Ali and, for one magic summer, her image possessed him in every waking moment. When she unwittingly made his life a living hell and yet knew that she was all he lived for.

Chris's wife reached for the stepladder and climbed out, graceful and lithe, unaware of being stared at. Alison watched the woman stroll towards the showers, before arms were suddenly wrapped around her legs as Shane and Sheila raced to greet her and her thoughts no longer had time to be her own.

⌖

Generally by Monday afternoon that pampered Fitzgerald's feeling would swamp Alison. The children were more settled in after their swim, but the boys still left mounds of food on their plates in their eagerness to escape and explore every corner of the gardens. Peadar would be back soon, dancing attention on her to compensate for his absence, and for now all she wanted was to take a good book and relax on the deckchair beside the crazy golf course in the gardens.

She could probably do without Chris Conway's family being there, if she was honest. But his presence didn't really perturb her now that she'd had time to adjust to it. She'd often wondered how his life had turned out. Curiosity was one of her pleasures and one of her faults. It might be fun to watch Chris now, no longer the youth who imagined himself unobserved as he sat like a lovesick calf on a bench shaded by trees opposite her bedsit on Drumcondra Road. Alison

57

wondered how he would introduce her to his wife. He could hardly call her an old girlfriend. They only ever kissed once and it was she who initiated that, a spontaneous, dare-devilish gesture as they climbed a steep road in Dalkey in late July sunshine on lunch break from the mobile van.

That was two weeks before the lunchtime on Lough-shinny beach, when she cut his hair, after which everything went sour. Alison never knew why she had pocketed a lock of his hair that day and kept it for years in an envelope. Maybe it was the intoxication of power. Chris was two years older than her, a year younger than Peadar. Yet if she had wanted to that lunchtime she could have cut off his beard or fingernails. She could have sheared him bald and he would have happily allowed it just to sense her body close to his.

His wife would know nothing of this and not even Peadar understood what had nearly happened in Loughshinny. Stated in black and white, she and Chris were never more than workmates, yet nothing about Chris was ever black and white. Possibly this mass of contradictions had given him his manic energy. He was always first up on the vans each morning, bowing like a head waiter to let the other staff enter, wise-cracking, drawing out shy newcomers, bullshitting half the time as he subverted every rule in the office. Then, if the van suddenly emptied so that they found themselves alone, he became tongue-tied, as unable to address her as he was unable to stop undressing her with his eyes.

Alison smiled as she settled back in her deckchair and urged Sheila not to cling on to her so much. Ever since being left in the pool this morning the girl was like a shadow. But Alison didn't really mind. A year or two ago Danny and Shane were the same, not allowing her a second to herself. Now part of her felt sad to watch them run freely around the grounds. Occasionally Shane tried to clamber onto rocks beside the ornate waterfall in the stream that wound between the crazy golf holes and she had to call him. But otherwise the boys could now be left to themselves.

Geraldine appeared in a tracksuit at the glass doors and started rounding up children for the afternoon's activities. The young woman's mood never changed from year to year. Good-tempered and amused by her charges, yet with her eyes only a fraction away from being thrown to heaven in mock horror. Danny was especially fond of her, and Alison watched him run to be first in the queue of children in mock formation. They would begin with clay modelling, she was saying, followed by multi-sports and then the great sandcastle-making competition on the beach.

In previous years Danny had been shy, but now he seemed eager to try everything and therefore Shane would tag along for a while as his shadow. But Alison knew the smaller boy would grow bored, especially if Danny latched onto somebody his own age and ignored him. She would need to check regularly that Shane wasn't just sitting among the other children, too shy to even cry.

Sheila had ventured into the sandpit beside the Slancy Room to play with the girl she'd met in the pool. They were setting up house in the giant-sized shoe there. Alison moved her chair slightly to keep an eye on her, then lay back to read while she got the chance.

Afternoon tea was being served when Peadar returned from the scramble. Older guests always queued in advance or gathered on armchairs near the serving counter like swallows in autumn. It had been her mother's favourite meal here. Not the extravagance of dinner, but the simple indulgence of being served tea and puff pastry cakes on a sofa. Alison smiled when she saw Peadar with a tray among the elderly couples. He grinned through the plate glass, holding up three fingers to show how many cakes he was going to fetch her. She shook her head vigorously, holding up a single finger but happily aware that he would ignore her. She could worry about her weight another day.

Peadar emerged into the sunshine and placed the loaded tray on the grass, making a great show of being her personal servant.

'Hurry up, slave,' she teased, 'or I'll beat you.'

'Promises, promises,' he laughed, lazing in the deckchair beside her and sipping his white coffee.

'How was the scramble?'

'Don't ask,' he replied. 'The Irwins stood too near the ball – after they hit it. The old lad had one moment of glory though, on the third. I hit the longest drive, but into the rough. We all scuffed the second shot so the best one was only trickled up the fairway. Then the guy chipped in from ninety yards. "An eagle, my first ever eagle," he kept scream- ing. I thought he was having a heart attack. I hadn't got it in me to remind him it was only a birdie and if his wife knew then she was singing dumb.'

'Was he cheating?'

'No. He was scrupulously honest for the rest of the round. Let him enjoy his glory.' He looked around. 'Where are the terrible threesome?'

Alison pointed towards Sheila and asked Peadar to check on Shane in ten minutes' time.

'Ten minutes,' he exclaimed. 'Did you ever think to see the day when we'd get ten minutes here to ourselves?'

It was nice to look back and laugh about the first year when Danny refused to stay in his high chair. They had been forced to eat meals hurriedly, taking turns to hold him down with one hand while Danny bawled and scattered place mats, spoons and anything else they could give him to play with. He was three before they could eat breakfast without a lump in their stomachs and by then Shane was unleashing spoons like an Olympic hammer-thrower.

Peadar stopped talking and looked towards the doors of the Slaney Room as Chris Conway emerged onto the patio. He nodded before strolling down the steps to the beach.

'You'll never guess who that is,' Alison said.

'Chris Conway.'

'Did you recognise him last night?' She was surprised. 'He's having the life of Riley here. I don't think I've seen him give his wife a hand with the kids once.'

'For Christ's sake, not so loud,' Peadar hissed.

'Well it's true,' Alison protested. 'I was fond of Chris, but his wife must be a right mouse.'

'She's dead.' Peadar's voice was low.

'What?'

'I meant to tell you when I got back, but I forgot. I heard about him at the scramble. He is supposed to play with some friends of the Irwins, so Jack Fitzgerald tipped them off at dinner last night. Seemingly Chris always brought his family here in the second week in June, but when he hadn't renewed his booking this year they let it go to someone else on the waiting list. He phoned last Tuesday and by a fluke they had a cancellation this week.'

'But . . .' Alison stopped. She had never actually seen Chris with the fair-haired woman. She had just presumed and linked them in her mind. What in God's name had she said in the steam room? Peadar glanced back, making sure the man didn't reappear on the steps.

'It happened in January,' he said. 'A head-on collision with another car on the Dunleer by-pass heading home from Dundalk. Their two daughters were killed as well, aged nine and twelve. Some young fellow on the wrong side of the road. The police had to cut all four dead bodies from the wreckage.'

Peadar picked up his coffee cup. Alison knew Chris Conway had returned. She heard the gate being bolted and waited for him to approach. She didn't know what she would say. She picked her book up, tempted to pretend she was absorbed in it, but knew that Peadar would find her behaviour odd.

'Hello, Chris,' she heard Peadar call.

'You're looking well, Peadar.' His voice was relaxed. She looked up but he was already past, strolling towards the first tee on the crazy golf course. He picked up a putter some child had dropped and they watched him aim a ball straight down the tunnel with the waterfall tumbling over it. He walked around to where his ball had stopped six inches from the hole, tapped in and walked on. Alison felt disturbed.

'What the hell is he doing here?'

'What do you mean?' Peadar replied. 'He has as much right to be here as anyone else.'

'And would you casually pop back here if I died? If we

were all killed?' Alison didn't know why she sounded this rattled. But it wasn't just the mistake of misreading the situation which upset her. This short break in Fitzgerald's was so precious that it seemed unfair to be forced to confront something so dark as this. She knew the thought was selfish, but just now she hadn't room to cope with somebody else's pain. There were three hundred and fifty-nine other days in the year when she would readily sympathise with any catastrophe.

'I don't know what I'd do if you died,' Peadar replied, looking at her. 'What the hell has got into you?'

Fitzgerald's must have been a place where Chris's family were happy, so how could he calmly face whatever memories confronted him in every corridor? She saw him in her mind, playing crazy golf with two laughing daughters. Alison watched him tee off on the second hole.

She felt cold. The other girl had left the sandpit and Sheila was digging alone in the sand. She came running when Alison called, delighted to be allowed to climb up onto her knee. Alison wished Chris Conway would go indoors or, better still, pack his bags and leave. Perhaps that was selfish, but Fitzgerald's wasn't meant to be about death. Two golden girls of nine and twelve, such perfect ages. Old enough to be independent, yet still happy in themselves before the guerrilla warfare of puberty.

She had been twelve when first kissed on the rock which still guarded the beach, a few steps away. Not that the rock looked anything like how she had seen it back then. Now it never seemed as large. Only twelve-year-old eyes could properly spy its grey and white streaks sparkling in the evening sun or experience the true sensation of sand pressing against bare soles.

Alison looked up and saw two boys emerge from the tennis courts. They stopped to watch Chris tackle the impossible slope of the Augusta hole. One said something and Chris handed him the putter. The boy narrowly missed and watched the ball roll back down the slope. He tried again and got it in one. The boy looked to be about twelve. He handed the putter back to Chris who walked towards the next hole that curved out of sight past a cluster of trees. There was nobody else on the course. The boys strolled carelessly on, already forgetting about Chris's existence.

That was how he had been every time she'd seen him here, she realised. Blending into the background, even when chatting to somebody. If he hadn't stared at her so blatantly, Alison knew she might never have been aware of his presence. Few people would notice his absence now if he simply kept walking after his ball, over the wall onto the roadway and back to Dublin. People were too preoccupied with their own lives, with growing families or growing old. Twenty years ago Chris stood out by perpetually alternating between manic exuberance and awkward shyness. Now she realised he had finally learnt the art of anonymously blending in.

'We should ask him to have a drink.' Peadar broke into her thoughts.

'Why?' She was suddenly defensive, unsure if Peadar had been watching Chris or observing her.

'Why not?' Peadar was puzzled. 'The poor guy is alone on holidays. He's obviously trying to rebuild his life but it can't be easy.'

'Maybe he wants to be left in peace.'

'This isn't like you,' Peadar probed. 'Normally you're full of concern for people. I mean at one time I half thought there was something going on between you.'

Alison laughed carefully. 'Sure, we were all only kids back then.'

'We were old enough.'

She knew what Peadar was thinking from his tone, even though they never discussed the child any more. She felt touched that the loss was still an ache inside him as well. Alison sensed his desire to take her hand, but he was afraid of being too blatant, in case he had mistaken her mood. He knew her too well though, knew how news of any child's death still upset her. It seemed crazy to draw comparisons though: Chris had lost the two children around whom he must have built his entire life. Years of caring and all his future hopes turning to dust before his eyes. Alison had only been eighteen and her feelings towards Peadar's baby inside her were mainly of fear at being thrust into motherhood when little more than a child herself. There was so much to deal with – her mother's disappointment, her father's resolute concern which couldn't disguise his hurt. She still remembered his bewilderment the evening they broke the news, like he was confronted by the second Immaculate Conception.

That was even before having to confront Peadar's mother who, when she was twenty-two, had received the gold medal in Greek when women students were rare in University College Dublin, and Peadar's father for whom she gave up her own ambitions to become the local headmaster's wife in Oughterard. Not that Alison had gone to Oughterard with

Peadar when he told them the news, but she had sensed their reaction from his silence on his return.

Yet neither family ever tried to push herself and Peadar into marriage. From the start her parents' advice was selfless, encouraging them to rush into nothing and let the child be born first. They had insisted that Alison would return to Waterford when eight months gone so they could mind her, and to hell with what the neighbours said. That night, crying in her old childhood bed (with Peadar bedded down on the sofa and her father and the dog asleep with one ear open), her pride in her parents' reaction only made her feel worse about herself. She was proud of Peadar too, who never thought of doing a runner, or at least gave no indication of thinking so.

It was Peadar who had insisted they tell her parents immediately, the evening they got the results from the clinic in Cathal Brugha Street. Otherwise Alison would have put it off, hiding in her bedsit to avoid going home until her father was forced to come and look for her. Peadar had travelled to Waterford with her when he could easily have stayed in Dublin. Her parents had never even heard about him before then. He took her hand when she was unable to find words and explained the situation himself, putting all blame firmly on his own shoulder.

The biggest shock was hearing her father address Peadar man to man: 'If I could get my hands on things in Waterford in the sixties I can't see why you couldn't have got them in Dublin now.' Alison had glanced at her mother who looked away. Back then she had been as shocked by the notion of her parents using condoms as if they had told her they had once been abducted by aliens. Condoms were still illegal in

Dublin and she was never sure how Peadar obtained them in St Patrick's Teacher Training College where he had impressed his tutors so much that he was being paid to teach foreign students there for the summer. For a horrified second she had thought that Peadar, in his defence, would describe how the condom burst inside her, but he had simply shaken his head and replied, 'I'm sorry, but I can't undo what's done.'

Maybe she had still been unsure of Peadar before then, or infatuated with him in an adolescent way. But during that evening she grew to depend on him to take control. Any thoughts she still harboured about Chris Conway vanished. Pregnancy overwhelmed her, turning her into a vulnerable child again. But it seemed to alter Peadar totally into an adult. She saw her parents grow to respect him, despite their anger. God knows how Chris Conway might have handled the situation.

Even when her diary confirmed that she was five days overdue, she still hadn't thought of Peadar or any man as her future husband back then. Certainly she was possessive of Peadar during that carefree summer, enjoying the status of going steady and fighting, often vainly, for his company and attention. But she had imagined years of freedom before the need for any full commitment. She had been her own woman and a free one. This was what had made her so angry with Chris, the fact that – from the moment he saw her in Peadar's company – he regarded her as somebody else's property. But she had belonged to nobody except herself. She was still there to be lost or won if Chris's shyness – or his notion of fundamental male decency – hadn't prevented him from crossing Peadar.

Chris came back into view, apparently bored of his

solitary golf. He stood on the windswept boardwalk, staring out to sea. She decided it wasn't fair to say her loss was nothing compared to his. It had been different, a minor tragedy, unnoticed, with no public mourning. Her child was seven weeks away from being born when Alison miscarried. That's what the doctor termed it, but in reality she had given birth to a stillborn girl. Nobody seemed to know exactly what to feel or how to behave. Of course there were displays of grief. Her mother had held her, both of them weeping. Peadar had wept too, saying she would have other children when the time was right. But all around she had sensed an overriding and unspoken feeling of relief.

The most frightening moment had been Peadar's mother visiting her unannounced in the hospital after the miscarriage. They had never met before, but the woman's very presence had cowed the nurses into leaving them alone even though visiting time was over. The headmaster's wife. The classical scholar. Alison knew the woman was reaching out to her, but the gulf was too great.

It was the first time Alison became aware that Peadar had had an elder brother, stillborn two years before him, and therefore unbaptised and buried — as was then the custom — in an unconsecrated strip of stony land near the sea. The woman had spoken for an hour about him, knowing perhaps that Alison was too intimidated to discuss her own feelings. Yet, even at that age, Alison sensed that Peadar's mother had probably never talked so openly about the stillbirth to anyone before. The image which haunted Alison was of Peadar as a child scrambling over rocks with his mother to reach that unmarked plot. So much weight cutting into his shoulders that they had been married for five years before Peadar ever told her the same story himself.

Alison had gone on to study nursing after the miscarriage – her mother having never taken her name off the list – mixing with new friends who knew nothing of her past. At the eleventh hour they had been reprieved, able to rebuild their lives, away from one another during the three years when she tried to escape from everything that brought back memories – before finding each other for the second time.

Yet none of that could explain why for years afterwards she broke into tears at the most unlikely moments. Watching a mother soothe a child at a bus stop or glimpsing an ad for nappies silently displayed on nine different screens in a television shop. It took her over a decade to make that one solitary visit to the Little Angels plot in Glasnevin Cemetery.

She had wheeled Danny past rows of white tombstones with the names of six children carved down each one, their ages listed in weeks and days, except for those born dead like her daughter. It had felt wrong to bring the child there, yet she had needed somebody with her and knew she could never ask Peadar. Instead of a reconciliation the visit had been more terrible than she could have imagined. Rows of sellotaped birthday cards along with teddies and toy cars littered each grave. Danny had started screaming, straining to reach the toy cars, while people tending other graves stared across, attracted by his cries. She had pushed the buggy on, starting to run before she ever located her daughter's name.

Alison fought against those memories now but couldn't prevent tears from welling up. Sheila touched her wet cheeks in alarm.

'Where do you hurt, Mammy?'

Alison passed the child across to Peadar. She stood up, knocking over cups as he called after her. She ignored him and ignored Shane who appeared in the doorway, being led back to them by Geraldine. She heard the boy call her and Peadar's voice coaxing Shane over to him instead. Alison opened the gate and walked quickly down onto the beach. She put her hand out to touch the rock. A virgin kiss at twelve. The brief blur of another six years and she had no longer been a virgin. A few months later she had been familiar with the aftertaste of death. It all seemed to happen in such a short space, yet the years since were an eternity. Why had Chris Conway to come and disturb her memories, here of all places?

Alison dried her eyes with her sleeve but tears came again. She stumbled over the sand, thankful the beach was empty. The tide was going out and soon this strand would be littered with teams of children building sandcastles as Geraldine laughed with the parents who came to watch. Evelyn, that was the name she'd chosen for her daughter. She would be eighteen now, perpetually rowing with her mother over clothes and make-up and boys, always ready to stick the knife in: 'You can't talk. At least I won't get banged up like you did at my age.' Alison could see her ghost daughter clearly, her skin, her teeth when she laughed, the very sheen of her black hair.

She hadn't felt the blues this badly since Sheila was born and Alison had toyed with the notion of calling her Evelyn. She swallowed hard, fighting for control. She was a grown woman on holidays, responsible for three children. Alison turned and saw Chris Conway on the boardwalk, watching.

She raised her hand, in some small gesture, although even she didn't understand what she wanted to convey.

You would swear Peadar was paying somebody to get their name known, Alison thought, as twice during the children's mealtime announcements came that he was wanted on the phone. On the first occasion he looked across the table and shrugged sheepishly.

'That has to be McCann,' she said, absolving him from his duty of pressurising Shane into finishing his sausages. 'You must have had the old buzzard time-locked in the safe until five o'clock so he can't call you every time the wall grows by another centimetre.'

She watched Peadar negotiate his way through children being fed on rows of straight-backed chairs that were far too grand for them. She loved this room with its 1930s landscapes and long tables laid out with party hats and napkins. This was where you met the other mothers properly, united in the effort of coercing children into tasting food when they were too excited to think of anything except playing. The mothers ranged from veterans with twelve-year-olds down to the flustered young woman beside Alison who introduced herself as Sally and whose baby kept screaming in his high chair. More food covered his bib than was reaching his mouth. Alison smiled to reassure Sally that everyone here had known far worse tantrums.

Joan waved from the far table. Alison smiled back. Monday night was free Irish coffee night, with dancing in the Slaney

71

Room while Joan dissected the pretensions of any over-dressed woman who passed. Alison walked across to Joan. She needed a laugh, even though she was over her fit of blues. Joan's kids ate everything before them, while their mother smoked, oblivious to any disapproval. Alison was still laughing at some story of hers when Peadar returned, worried-looking.

'What is it, pet?' she asked, going back to him. He shook his head.

'I'll tell you again.' He disappeared, taking Shane and Danny out for desserts while Sheila tentatively toyed with a homemade yoghurt. But before the boys even returned with their toffee crunch ice creams Peadar's name was called again on the PA system. This time he was gone much longer and the children's disco had started in the Slaney Room before he returned.

Danny was too big to still be jumping around with the tiny tots, falling down to wave his feet when the music stopped. But he did so automatically and unselfconsciously, lured by the prospect of medals on Thursday evening – even though he knew by now that every child got one, regardless of what they did. Sheila was too young to be self-conscious. She danced away, imitating her elder brother, while Shane sat stubbornly beside Alison, content to watch but refusing to join in.

Peadar touched her shoulder and she turned in her armchair, startled.

'You look worried,' she said. 'It's nothing to do with the house or anyone ill, is it?'

'It's the extension,' Peadar replied. 'Look, I need to slip off and have a think. I might take a sauna even. Is that okay?'

She nodded and watched him walk towards the leisure centre. If Peadar wasn't willing to talk about something, then it must be bad. She knew he was upset. The sauna and steam room would be quiet now, with just a few parents skipping off or older couples. She didn't like to think of him lying on a towel, with sweat pouring from his body as he tried to solve whatever problem McCann had now landed on him.

Sheila had grown tired of dancing and wandered off to play among empty tables at the edge of the dance floor. Alison glanced around to keep an eye on her and spotted Chris Conway alone on a stool at the bar. He summoned the barman with a flick of his finger to pour another Irish Mist liqueur, then lit a cigar from a packet on the counter and watched the lithe bodies of the dancing children. He seemed unaware of being stared at. Nobody paid him any heed but she wished he would stop looking at Danny. Shane had slipped away to watch the dancers from beside the stage, like a child afraid of water but tentatively dipping one toe in a pool. She willed him to find the courage to dance, but he seemed trapped by his inhibition, unable to move.

That was how Chris Conway had frequently looked during that distant summer when his feelings became obvious towards her. The jester caged by self-doubt and shyness. She glanced back again. It was impossible to know what he was thinking. His eyes had a resigned calmness with a half smile on his lips. Maybe it was something primeval and super-stitious within her, but she felt the sight of these joyous children was a private one for parents only and he had now ceased to be one. He had no cause to be here, no one left to watch over. If he had an ounce of natural feeling then how could he bear to calmly sit here like a Jonah, she wondered?

Chris noticed her. He smiled and nodded. Alison looked back at the dancers, embarrassed at being caught. She would have to go over and apologise for what she'd said in the steam room. Geraldine stopped the music and arranged the children around her for their nightly renditions of *Twinkle, Twinkle, Little Star* and *The Barney Song*. Alison knew she was being unfair, but how could Chris listen to those voices and watch their bright eyes as they held the mike? Surely he would leave once the singing started. But she refused to turn and check. A young father knelt to photograph his daughter who sang with a faltering voice. A mother stretched her arms out towards her son who had finished. Alison wondered what the hell could be so bad as to make McCann telephone the hotel twice.

The songs ended. Geraldine called on Danny to lead the train of children parading down to the video room. Shane ran to be second in line, then made room for Sheila to squeeze between them as other children formed carriages. Danny glanced at Alison warningly, making sure she knew that she was expected to follow. She indicated she would do so shortly, then glanced behind. Chris was in conversation with the barman, seemingly oblivious to the children now. She had five minutes' grace before Danny started searching for her. Alison slipped down the passage into the leisure centre. Both pools were empty and the jacuzzi deserted when she looked in through the glass. She wondered whether Peadar was in the steam room or sauna or maybe back in their room. Alison waited for as long as possible, hoping he would come out.

She couldn't explain this sudden desperate need to catch a glimpse of him.

Peadar was on the phone when she brought the kids back to get ready for the babysitter. He looked up when she came in, muttered, 'I'll get back to you,' and put the receiver down.

'What the hell is happening?' she asked. 'Are you on holidays with us or still running that school? Surely whatever it is can wait till we get home?'

'That might be sooner than you think,' Peadar replied, quietly so that none of the children overheard. They were too preoccupied anyway, trying to find the in-house video channel on television to watch the end of their film.

'What do you mean?' she whispered, noticing his shoulders stooped like an old man's. 'What's wrong with that bloody extension now?'

'There won't be a bloody extension,' Peadar said, 'or at least not for a long time yet. The builder has gone bust. I knew Nolan was juggling three or four jobs but I didn't know how badly over-stretched he was.'

'Oh, poor Peadar.' Alison sat on the bed beside him, longing to take him in her arms, yet not wanting the children to sense anything was amiss. All his years of work, of fundraising and loans, and some bastard could simply cheat him out of it.

'His workmen walked off the site at half-four, leaving the place a mess,' Peadar said. 'Cement literally stiffening in the wheelbarrows where they abandoned them. It wasn't just that they realised their wages weren't going to be paid, I think half of them were illegal and didn't wait around to answer questions. McCann says there isn't even a security man to watch over the scaffolding tonight and suppliers keep arriving, trying to remove materials they claim weren't paid for.'

'That's terrible.' Alison took his hand, shocked to feel a tremor there. If she stroked his chest she knew she would be able to feel his heart thumping like a trapped bird. 'What can you do?'

'I don't know, but I can't leave things the way they are.'

'Well, you can hardly start rolling up your sleeves and mixing cement,' she replied. His voice didn't sound like his own, with all the fight knocked from it. Peadar, her rock, who needed her. She worried about his heart and hated the children seeing him this upset. 'It's not your fault.'

'When you're a headmaster, everything is your fault,' he said. 'Like my father always says, it comes with the job. I'll have to go back in the morning.'

This time Danny overheard. Alison spied the boy, sitting very still on his bed. Then his lip began to quiver and suddenly he was crying, setting off the younger two, even though they didn't know what was happening.

'We're going nowhere, we're staying here,' Danny shouted. 'This is our holiday.'

'Of course you can stay,' Peadar tried reassuring him. 'Your Daddy will just have to pop home for a night or so. Mammy will be here with you and everything else will be just the same.'

A knock came, the babysitter arriving early. Of course it wouldn't be the same, Alison thought, nothing would be the same. It would be no holiday for her. She looked at Peadar who shook his head. This wasn't the time to argue, they would have all evening for that. Sheila was still crying and Shane was upset too. They needed to put up a cheerful front or leave three sobbing children with the babysitter, who, thankfully, was a mature woman with grown-up children. If she sensed the tension she didn't let on, making a great fuss of Sheila and getting Shane to show her his colouring.

Soon the youngest two were excited again, bringing the woman books for bedtime reading. Only Danny remained uneasy. Alison noticed how his giraffe was carefully placed on the floor beside his bed – far enough away that it might belong to Shane, but within reach for him to cuddle into when the babysitter turned the light out. He looked up at Alison suspiciously as she kissed him. All year long he would talk to her about Fitzgerald's. She knew that these five days stretched before him like a paradise which nothing must be allowed to disturb.

'We're going nowhere,' he hissed fiercely, holding tears back. She kissed him again and stroked his hair.

'Of course not,' she whispered. 'You read your book and get to sleep soon. I'll talk to Daddy and sure maybe he won't have to go at all.'

———— ◦◦◦ ————

*I'll talk to Daddy.* The words mocked her, walking down the corridor in silence. This was the night when she had meant to talk to him, to tell Peadar her worries from the previous months. She knew it was childish to have looked forward to being told how brave she was and scolded for keeping the tests from him. But she had fantasised so often about what she would say and Peadar's reaction to it. When she closed her eyes during those tests she had even been able to conjure up the taste of Irish coffees and the smoke from his cigar.

What was the point in saying anything now? Her false alarm seemed meaningless compared to his loss that could be measured in tangible bricks and mortar and vanished money.

The dining room was filling up, a warm hubbub of noise greeting them as they waited to be seated. She looked around, wondering in which alcove Jack Fitzgerald seated Chris Conway every evening. She knew from Peadar's face that he had already slipped back into his school principal mode. The relaxation she'd seen there after his golf was gone, the mood in which she felt she had him all to herself. She wondered if Peadar had personally gone guarantor for anything, if their house could be at risk. It didn't seem likely but during these last weeks Peadar would have signed anything to get this job completed. Even this holiday stretched their finances, with hopes of a new kitchen abandoned for another year at least.

They didn't discuss the subject over their starter or soup, as if trying to keep some outward semblance of a holiday alive. Peadar chose the Chianti Classico Grande Reserva he would normally keep as a treat until their final night. She looked across at him as the waiter removed the bisque he had barely touched.

'I've no choice,' he said quietly. 'I have to go.'

'I know.' She reached for his hand, knowing Peadar would sort out the pieces of this mess, slowly and methodically, like he had done with their lives after she lost the child. At first she hadn't allowed him to, by running away, trying to pretend it had never happened. But his healing came during the nights before they married when he had held her and allowed the tears to come. His calmness was vital, when she spent her life perpetually flying off the handle, perched in mid-air between tears and elation. But Peadar wasn't so young any more. She had to mind him.

'Let's cancel the holiday,' she suggested. 'We can have a word with Jack Fitzgerald. Maybe he'll find us a summer cancellation.'

'How?' Peadar asked. 'A long-standing guest virtually has to die before you get a summer slot here. There's no way I can take a week off during term time and we haven't the money anyway. The kids have been looking forward to this all year, so we can't drag them home.'

'Tell me the truth, Peadar,' she said. 'I won't get upset. Have we lost any money ourselves?'

He looked at her blankly. 'What do you mean?'

'I mean, are any of our savings mixed up in the money the school is after losing?'

'The school isn't after losing money,' he replied. 'Obviously the job was bonded.' He saw her puzzled stare. 'Before a job like this starts, myself and the builder enter into a bond with a bank. Basically I lodge the money up front to prove I have it and the bank holds onto it to pay the builder once the job is completed. As soon as the courts appoint a receiver, we can fix an amount to pay for work done so far, then put the remainder of the job out to tender.'

She could tell that Peadar was baffled by her expression. Even she was unsure whether to feel relief or anger.

'So you mean the blasted extension will get built after all?'

'Not immediately. We'll lose a few months but it will get done.'

'So all you've really lost is time.'

'I wouldn't go that far,' he explained patiently. 'In addition to disruption there will be other expenses, legal fees and so forth. But once I sniffed danger I made sure to keep a close eye on Nolan.'

'So what will you be doing in Dublin?'

'Talking to the solicitors, though I've already filled them in on the phone. Then setting up meetings for next week and generally being a presence around the place.' He stopped. 'Why are you looking at me like that?'

'A presence around the place?' she repeated, incredulously. 'McCann is a presence around the place. He's been a presence in our bloody marriage for years. You say these meetings are for next week. I know this has sent your precious plans haywire, but what exactly can you do in Dublin between now and Friday that you couldn't do with a few phone calls from here?'

'That's not the point.'

She knew Peadar wanted her to keep her voice down. The couple at the next table had ceased their own conversation, their stiffened shoulders betraying the fact that they were listening. Jack Fitzgerald was seven tables away and closing. Peadar glanced in his direction.

'What is the point?' she asked.

'The point is that I'm school principal, captain of the bloody ship. As my father says, if there's trouble I'm suppose to be on deck, strapped to the wheel.'

'You're not your bloody father,' Alison snapped.

'What's that supposed to mean?'

It was an old argument, one Alison didn't want to get side-tracked into. 'You often work till after midnight,' she said. 'Nobody doubts your commitment. So what's so important to prove that you can't take five nights off to reintroduce yourself to your family?'

'Don't exaggerate.' Jack Fitzgerald had skipped tables and was now only one away. 'It would be taken badly if I didn't show my face. I'll try to get back down for Thursday night. There'll be other holidays, I'll make this up to you, I promise.'

He tried to squeeze her hand but she withdrew it, clenching her fist in frustration under the table. Part of her knew he was right, but she wanted him, just for once, to shag his precious commitments and put her first. He had needed her so badly once. That had been a terrible shock to discover when he came looking for her again after three years, to find how this strong confident figure desperately needed her in his life. So why couldn't he show it now, or had that vulnerability faded with the years?

'There are lots of people you know here,' he reassured her. 'I'll talk to Jack and make sure the staff treat you like a queen.'

'I don't want to be left alone,' she protested. 'It won't be a holiday.'

'It will be for the kids.'

Peadar looked up as Jack Fitzgerald reached their table, his hands joined in front of him, leaning down, anxious to ensure their comfort. It had taken her years to adjust to this routine of senior Fitzgerald's staff moving between the tables every evening. It was embarrassing if her mouth was full when somebody stopped, yet she could never bring herself to stop eating when one of them drew near in case it looked like she was seeking attention.

Jack listened carefully as Peadar outlined the situation. Arrangements were being smoothly made between them. Alison knew she would be waited on hand and foot. Jack was the fourth generation of his family to own the hotel. There was nothing he hadn't seen before, nothing which ever perturbed him. It was nobody's fault that he had appeared just now at their table, but she resented the fact that she had never finished her conversation with Peadar who gave the impression of everything being decided between them. A waitress was named to help her at the lunch buffet. Geraldine would be asked to give the children extra attention. Jack even foresaw the difficulty of the boys getting changed in the leisure centre.

Peadar's mood was improving with every moment. The analytical side of his brain was at work, breaking her holiday down into a series of logistical problems. She longed to kick him under the table and suggest he arrange a gigolo as well, for good measure, or for a life-size rubber replica of himself to be erected on the tennis courts that she could take her frustrations out on with a baseball bat. She wanted him to stop planning her life, so she cut in, asking Jack about Chris Conway instead.

'You know him?' Jack Fitzgerald sounded surprised.

'He worked with Alison years ago,' Peadar said. 'Had a soft spot for her, if I remember, though it was harmless adolescent stuff.'

Jack Fitzgerald laughed politely, taking his lead from Peadar, so that Alison felt forced to laugh along, though by now she was truly angry. Could that really be how Peadar remembered it? If Chris's feeling were adolescent, then what were Peadar's own feelings back then? Perhaps he had always viewed her as a set of logistical problems to be solved, so confident of his own strength that he never felt the need to be concerned about the attentions of anyone as hesitant as Chris Conway.

'We were thinking of inviting him for a drink later on,' Peadar said. 'I mean, does it help him to talk about the accident?'

'I get the impression he just wants a quiet holiday,' Jack Fitzgerald advised, discreet and circumspect as always when asked about any guest. 'I think he's going away afterwards, leaving Ireland as far as I know. His house is up for sale in Dublin. I'd tread carefully if I were you. I never expected to see him here again, but when he phoned last Tuesday he wanted everything exactly the same, even down to the room. He offered to pay extra because it was a family room on the ground floor corridor, just down from yours. But I refused the money. I've warned a few guests who might remember him, in case they put their foot in it. But I think the man just wanted to come back one last time for his own reasons and is happier to have no fuss.'

Jack moved on to the next table and Peadar noticed her look.

'What is it?' he asked.

'Nothing.'

'Don't "nothing" me. I had to arrange things when I got the chance. I've a meeting with the solicitors at half-nine tomorrow.'

'When did you arrange that?'

'On the phone.'

'Before checking with me? Before we discussed a single thing?'

Her anger sounded tired and soured by a hundred petty grievances. It wasn't even directed at Peadar. He was the man he always would be. Absolutely correct in his absolutist world which made more sense than her intuitive one. It was herself she was angry with, for expecting him to be someone different. Maybe he was and she just couldn't see it. The hours he spent since his mother's death in his office in the spare room demanding not to be disturbed. The way he threw himself into this school building project. Was it simply a way to avoid dealing with his family or dealing with himself, his ageing, the disappointments blunting any life? She knew uncles like that in Waterford, men who kept building onto their family homes even after their families left. Perpetually mixing cement, digging foundations, anything to avoid having to venture indoors to their wives.

Peadar was patiently explaining how he had no choice. The scaffolding was an insurance danger. People would keep arriving until he secured the site with the receiver. Alison found herself switching off. She might have been watching a goldfish, they lived in such different worlds at times. That dream image came back, the woman trapped at the porthole of a capsized ship. Surely to God herself and Peadar were happy, but was she sure?

Her friend Ruth was sure until she found that her husband had been meeting another woman for two years. Peadar wasn't like that, but sometimes now Alison didn't know what he was like, what inarticulate hurts he carried inside. Peadar, beaten by his father in class to show there was no favouritism. Picking fights against older boys, getting battered just to try and prove himself to his classmates. Peadar, who had to drink harder, play harder, chase girls harder and was still treated with the same suspicion as the local sergeant's son. For him Dublin had been a far greater escape from a cage than it was for her. He ceased his monologue.

'Do you understand?' he asked.

'Yes,' she replied, knowing it would do no good. He was off again, justifying his decision as much to himself as to her. How McCann was incapable of doing a headmaster's job, but resented the fact that anybody else could. He would be secretly thrilled by the chance to tell everybody how his own misgivings were overruled. But the more Peadar repeated himself the more Alison sensed that at heart he knew he could stay here if he put his foot down. Surely his return to Dublin couldn't be over anything as childish as a dread of what his father would say when he finally phoned Oughterard with the news? Peadar looked at her sharply.

'I'm thinking ten years down the road,' he explained. 'University, colleges abroad, the sort of money we'll need. Things have to go smoothly if I'm to land a better job elsewhere. I want our kids to be able to afford any course they're good enough for. This is what fathers do, you know.'

More jobs, more targets, more points to prove. I gave up my happiness to make another person happy, she thought.

At twenty-two the responsibility of Peadar's need had overwhelmed her when they got back together. This assured young man reduced to tears as he talked about his loneliness in the years since she left him. The cramming he had done for his finals, getting straight As in everything, except for a B in art. How his mother had sighed when he phoned home and just said, 'What a terrible pity about the art.' That first night they got back together again it had taken hours before he finally came inside her, like he was all clenched up, as if nobody had ever taught him how to let go. 'You wouldn't care if I was a roadsweeper,' he used to say. 'You don't know how kind you are to people. You're not even aware of your specialness.'

Yet she had never felt special, except with Chris, before Peadar said that. His words had made her feel so truly loved that she never took time to question her own love for him. Perhaps it was inevitable that married life never quite matched the intensity of those first months. This wasn't true, she told herself, she was reinventing the past. Everything was upsetting her, the ruined holiday, even Chris Conway's presence. Peadar was her rock, chipped around the edges, but still the only person she could trust. It would be nice if he was happier, but the gnawing disappointment was with himself and not her. She reached across to touch his fingers.

'I understand,' she lied. 'But let's not have that drink with Chris tonight. Let's just talk instead.'

They didn't though. They sat in silence, nursing their Irish coffees. How could she begin to tell him about her health fears that had come to nothing and therefore proved unnecessary? He would respond all right but no matter what he said it would never be enough. It was like the kids' reaction to their arrival here. She always seemed to want more than people could give.

Peadar wanted her body. All the way up the corridor

she could sense his need. An empty house awaited him in Dublin, with pre-packed microwaved meals as he dealt with problems. In bed in the dark she could feel him waiting for a sign, for her to turn and run her hand down his bare chest. When none came his fingers stroked her hair. They stopped, feeling her wet cheeks.

'You're crying. I'm sorry, Alison, I hate to make you cry.'

How could she tell Peadar that he wasn't the reason she was crying? Ever since turning the light out it wasn't his face she was imagining. It was Chris Conway's, lying in an empty room down the corridor. His wife, what must she have looked like? His daughters laid out on mortuary slabs. The anguish and pity she had kept in check all day came rushing in. Peadar held her as she sobbed, soothing her, promising that he would make up for everything. She could see the wrecked cars meshed together, the funeral with three coffins, the bedrooms of toys and clothes to be cleared out.

She wanted to tell Peadar about her grief but how could she start talking about another man? She wanted him to make love to her, even as she cried. To climb on top and take control, forcing her back into their own world. But he was too concerned, too guilty about abandoning her in the morning.

When she finally stopped crying, he lay curled with his arm paternally around her. She feigned sleep so he would get some, then lay awake, listening. Those special holiday sounds. Wind among the trees in the gardens, the distant waves beyond and then, when she was almost asleep, the same solitary footsteps she had heard pass along the gravel on Sunday night. She found herself trying to stay awake, perturbed and anxious to hear if they returned. But sleep overcame her and when she woke, Peadar was already dressed. It was six a.m., with grey light fringeing the curtains. She wanted to call him back into bed but mentally he was already gone.

'I'll phone you,' he whispered. 'It's better the kids don't see me go.'

'Drive safely. Take your time. There are lunatics on the road.'

He nodded. She knew he was torn inside. The toughness was gone. He didn't want to leave. For half a moment she thought he would find the courage to turn back.

'I'll make it up to you,' he said.

His father's reluctant son. She prayed that the roads would be safe, the light good. 'Phone when you reach the house, the moment you get home.'

Peadar kissed her, then looked across at his children, afraid to wake them by venturing too close. He picked up his bag and left, quietly closing the door.

# TUESDAY

Alison didn't imagine she would sleep again after Peadar left, but she must have because suddenly Danny was in bed beside her, angrily hissing, 'Where is he? Where's Daddy after going?'

The room was still dark but only because the heavy curtains were drawn. Her stomach felt sick with tiredness and stress. She hated it when Danny surprised her like this, asking awkward questions before her eyes were even open. She held him tight, trying to quieten him and get him on her side before he woke the others.

Shane and Sheila would take their cue to Peadar's departure from his reaction but it was Danny who flew most easily into tears and tantrums. The prospect of the days ahead frightened her. What if one of the children got sick or she was simply unable to cope?

'You have to help me, Danny,' she said. 'It's you and me in charge now.' The boy stared back, momentarily flattered by the prospect of authority, then started to cry. Not angrily this time, but curled away from her in a ball.

'What is it, pet? Tell me.'

'Nothing. Leave me alone.'

Sheila was awake now. Maybe she'd been awake the entire time. She snuggled down into Alison's arms, quiet in herself, asking nothing. Danny turned over, his face wet, keeping a slight distance.

'Do we have to go home too?'

'Of course not. We'll have the best holiday ever.'

He put his arms around her. The crying stopped, but she knew that paradise had been tainted for him, the security of the perfect rhythm he seemed to need on this holiday. She worried for him, not just now but in the future. How could he ever cope with the imperfect adult world that would be strewn before him like pieces of a clock taken apart and never quite fitting back together again?

———— ❧ ————

Breakfast was surprisingly easy. The children relished the novelty of being different, with Shane babbling away to everyone that their Daddy was missing on secret business. Jack Fitzgerald had done his work and the staff fussed around them. It was cloudy, the patio wet after rain. After eating, she put their coats on and let them wander in the gardens, while she sat at the open French doors of their room, anxious for the phone to ring.

The radio news was on in case of road accidents. She wasn't happy until Peadar called just before ten, but even then he couldn't talk as he was in the solicitor's office. Still it was enough to know he was safe, after all the recent dawn crashes on the N11 with people speeding for the ferry.

Shane came in, complaining that Danny had made new friends and wouldn't let him play. Alison let him help her gather up the swim gear, then set out to find the others. Sheila was in the sandpit with her friend from yesterday. Danny sat on the seesaw with two Galway brothers, obviously twins. All three clammed up as she approached.

As they walked to the pool she scolded Danny for excluding Shane. The attendant was waiting, ready to bring Danny into the gents' changing room where a curtained cubicle was reserved. Shane wanted to go in too, but she knew the boy couldn't dry himself properly afterwards. She warned Danny to stay in the shallow end, while she struggled to get herself and the younger ones ready.

It took ten minutes, between blowing up armbands, then getting annoyed when they refused to wait for her. Alison couldn't stand being hurried. It made her go slower. She had forgotten to bring plain soap for Sheila and would have to use perfumed gel on her skin. None of them were talking by the time they emerged to find Danny playing donkey with one of the twins, tossing a float over the heads of some smaller children.

She made him stop before anyone got hurt, insisting he play with Shane. The boys moved off, Danny towing Shane behind him like a ball and chain. Alison played ring-a-rosy with Sheila, lifting the laughing child out of the water. The pool was filling up. Jets of foam bubbled up from the under-water ledge at the shallow end where toddlers climbed. She sat back, letting the foam wash around Sheila and herself. The child feigned fear and wriggled away, seeing her new friend walk down the pool steps. Heinrich Diekhoff waded carefully in behind her, patiently watched over by his father.

Alison stretched her legs and yawned, then saw Chris Conway sitting at the poolside. It was ridiculous trying to avoid him. She smiled to him and he lowered himself into the water and waded across.

'Chris, I want to apologise,' she began.

'Why?'

'Yesterday, in the steam room, I didn't know your circumstances. I said the wrong thing.'

'That's all right.' He eased himself onto the ledge beside her. 'Sure I wouldn't know what to say myself.'

'How are you coping?' The question sounded mundane.

'Okay. How are you?'

'Not so good. Peadar had to go home. A builder doing work at the school went bust.'

Even as she spoke, she knew that, comparatively, her problems were minor. But she had a life of her own.

'That will be hard,' he sympathised. 'Alone with three kids who seem real livewires.'

'What were your girls called?' she inquired. 'Or should I ask? I'm sorry, I don't know what I should avoid asking.'

'Rachel and Sara,' he replied. 'And Jane, my wife. You would have liked her.'

'I'm sorry.'

'That's okay.' He looked around at the children splashing.

'Were they fond of Fitzgerald's?'

'They loved it. Jane came here as a kid, but it was well out of my league when I was growing up.'

'Mine too,' she said. 'You've obviously done well.'

'I'd a good partner. He understood business and I understood what we made money from. Vanity and greed.'

'I thought Peadar mentioned the book trade.'

'The remainder business. Why anyone would be vain enough to write a book I don't know. You walk into warehouses packed to the gills with unsold hardbacks from the latest bright young thing. Auctioned off at a few pence each.

94

Then, at the other end, you have punters forking out for books they don't want, tempted by the thought of getting a bargain.'

'It sounds sad.'

'It's human nature, Ali.'

'Don't call me Ali.'

'I'm sorry.'

'It's just that I never used the name again. It makes me sound like somebody else.'

Chris smiled. 'You look the same Ali to me.'

Alison stretched her toes out, hoping Sheila would rescue her. She had apologised for the steam room. Now twenty years seemed too long to try and renew a friendship. 'Why don't you swim where there's space in the big pool?' she asked.

'I wish I could.' Chris laughed. 'But sure I can't swim a stroke.'

She remembered watching him dive into the plunge pool, his seeming lack of fear, and felt unsure whether to believe him.

'Do your kids like books?' he asked.

'Yes.'

His toes were inches from hers. She wondered if he remembered the intense games of footsie they once played while serving customers at the library counter.

'I must look in my van. I usually have samples, though I'm not sure what's there since I sold my share of the business.'

'What do you do now?' Alison lowered her feet away from his.

She had known she would meet Chris this morning. It

was why she had changed her bathing costume from the one she wore yesterday.

'There're only so many book auctions you can sit through,' he said, skirting the question. 'Especially in the States where you pick up Irish books for nothing. I remember coming home from my first trip there. Rachel – she was only five – found an illustrated edition we'd bought of *The Old Man and the Sea*. Printed in Thailand, with that smell you get off shiny paper there. One picture was of the old man's palms torn open by ropes. She made me tell her the whole story, how the sharks get the fish and all. She kept the book beside her bed for a year. Every night she'd kiss the man's hands to make them better.'

Sheila swam towards them, slowly, in her armbands. Chris's story disturbed Alison, its intimacy making her unsure how to respond. She willed Sheila to swim faster.

'She sounds a nice kid.' Alison found that she couldn't use the past tense.

'You can't teach kindness,' Chris replied. 'Kids have it or they don't. Even in sleep Rachel looked kind, especially asleep.'

He went silent and Alison sensed his sudden desire to be away, anonymous again. Sheila reached them and threw herself into Alison's arms. She looked at Chris.

'Who are you?'

'Just a man.'

His foot touched Alison's under the water. She was about to be annoyed, then saw that he was discreetly drawing her attention to Shane leaning dangerously over the empty Jacuzzi, trying to dip a float into the bubbling froth.

Alison grabbed Sheila and rose, disturbed that it was Chris who had spotted the danger. She was Shane's mother and he didn't even have children any more. She was shocked by the cruelty of the thought even as she ran to grab Shane before he tumbled in. As she scolded him, she knew her anger was with herself. Yet it was true. Chris seemed like an impostor, casting a hex over the happy families in the water.

The teenage Dublin girls laughed with their father in the adult pool, oblivious to how his stupidity might have killed them all. She turned but Chris had already vanished. An elderly woman lowered herself into the water for her daily lesson with the gentle instructor who seemed just as old as her. Maybe it was the plastic bathing cap, but Alison felt this same woman had been here every year, perpetually relearning her awkward doggy paddle. This was Fitzgerald's Hotel, a continuum existing outside time, an uninterrupted pattern forever and ever.

She shivered as she closed her eyes, suddenly holding onto the Jacuzzi rail. The images were so clear she couldn't blot them out, one car meshed into another, bodywork compressed like a concertina. Glass everywhere, flecked with specks of blood. The blood of somebody's children, somebody's wife. An unknown woman who, in some way, had been her rival; whose naked body must have been compared against her unglimpsed one; whose laughter and smile were weighed against the memory of hers.

Sheila pulled at her hand, urging her back into the pool. The boys were already in, calling. She saw Chris emerge from the showers. He took a towel and crossed towards the steam room. A woman coming out held the door open as he made

97

a joke and she smiled back, then walked on, already forgetting him.

Shane climbed impatiently from the water and jumped into her arms. He wrapped himself around her, her rebuke already forgotten. She could smell chlorine in his hair. His happiness was almost tangible, like a force field glowing around him. How precious and short this time was. She carried him down the pool steps. Danny clambered onto her back, causing her to stagger in the water which splashed into her eyes, momentarily blinding her. Both boys hugged her, their laughter in her ears as they pulled her down so that she choked on the chlorine. The boys found room for Sheila in the embrace too, their feet twirling her around. Alison was a good swimmer but suddenly panicked, as if there was something in the water that she couldn't protect them from.

It was two girls' faces she kept seeing, aged nine and twelve, one thrown across the other's lap as firemen cut the roof away. Alison seemed to be above them, staring down. Even the diverted traffic edging past made no noise as ambulancemen knelt with blankets to cover up the woman's body they had cut free. Water stung Alison's eyes again as Danny and Shane laughed and kicked out. Sheila giggled too, a hymn of happiness encircling her until they were suddenly gone.

Alison opened her eyes, gasping for breath, and heard a loud splash as the waterfall came on, attracting children like a magnet. She knew Danny would swim right through it, while Sheila watched and Shane edged himself carefully along the tunnel between the sheet of water and the wall.

She watched them, her face so wet that even she couldn't tell if she'd been crying. A nine-year-old's face unmarked until you lifted her head and found the skull was cracked. Where were these details coming from? Maybe she had seen news footage, yet she had no recollection of the accident. There were so many photos of twisted wreckage in the paper, so many horror statistics reported that you simply blocked them out.

She checked the clock. Half-twelve. Already families would be queuing for lunch in the Slaney Room, while older couples were waited upon in the dining room. She would need a window table, close to the playroom and overlooking the gardens. That way she could keep an eye on all three. Chris's tragedy wasn't hers, so why was it affecting her like this? She had to pull herself together and organise the children. They would protest, with Sheila crying at having to get out of the pool. She hardly knew why she bothered. They would pile up their plates, then eat almost nothing, too excited by life, blessed at having so much new to see and experience.

But she knew she would drag them from the pool any-way, find a table and the waitress Jack Fitzgerald had promised. She would cajole them into eating something, mop up the milk they knocked over and finally set them free. Her own lunch would be cold by then and her temper frayed, but none of that mattered. This was what a mother did in the here and now world that you learnt to exist in.

———— ✣ ————

She was glad not to see Chris again during lunch. Once Danny finished eating he paired off with the Galway twins, united by a shared fascination with Enid Blyton stories. They bent their heads together in huddled whispers, deciding which guests were villains, linked in a conspiracy. Alison wondered if the RTE executive realised they were trailing him, flitting between trees, while he earnestly practised for Thursday's crazy golf competition.

Before each holiday she worried about them making friends, but Danny's newly-invented gang was a concern too, as she could see Shane being left out. His mind was too practical to sneak behind adults, then report back to secret meetings. Besides, part of the excitement in any Secret Seven adventure was inventing passwords and Alison knew that, for Danny and the twins to feel they belonged to something special, they needed somebody to keep out.

Several times she found Shane wandering around lost, looking for Danny, when she knew they were hiding from him. Not only was he too small to be alone, but she hated his bewildered look. She was relieved when Geraldine took the children down onto the beach early. But even there she saw the three of them refuse to let him help build their sand-castles, though she knew Shane had such an individual way of doing everything that he would end up destroying their carefully arranged moats and fortresses.

Sheila took one look at the beach and ran back, clinging to her. But Alison was glad of her company. She stood on the steps, holding Sheila in her arms, wishing she had a hat for the child who seemed strangely bothered by the sun. Shane was happy, pottering around on his own, but she couldn't stop watching over him. Sand brushed against her lips. Children passed up and down in their bare feet. The loudspeaker announced a phone call for Room 103. Out at sea the ferry from France was arriving. Shane looked up and saw her. He dropped his spade and came running. Sheila clambered from her arms, ready for her favourite game with her brother. They ran towards the crazy golf course, pushing their balls along with a putter, picking them up when they spun back down the slopes and using their palms to cup them into the holes.

They raced on, laughing. Alison's book lay on a deck-chair. She sat down and, keeping one eye on them, tried to read. But she couldn't focus. The images from the pool still haunted her. She imagined herself at the wheel. At what stage did Chris's wife know they were going to die? Time inside a crash must surely be different. A second could stretch to eternity with everything startlingly clear as the other car loomed up, as you braked hard and knew it was not enough, as you watched the impact occur in measured stages, each frame of time crawling forward while you slowly cried your children's names.

Alison looked up. The old lady who had received swimming lessons was watching her.

'You should get a cardigan with that wind, love,' she said. 'You don't even know you're shivering.'

Alison told Shane and Sheila she was returning to the room, knowing they would soon follow to watch cartoons. But she was glad of the few moments alone as she sat on the bed and phoned their house in Dublin.

The answering machine came on, with Peadar's measured voice. She didn't leave a message, not wanting Peadar to think she was chasing him. She phoned the school. McCann answered and she put the phone down. The last thing she wanted was to speak to him and she knew that Peadar could never be himself when talking in somebody else's presence.

What did she want to say to Peadar anyway? If she couldn't cope with these first few hours alone, then how would she manage until Friday? Peadar had enough stress without her irrational foreboding. Sheila and Shane ran into the room, pulling their sneakers off, spilling out mounds of sand onto the polished floorboards. Shane found the remote control and they both settled back happily on a bed.

Alison took her book and sat outside on the gravel path beyond the French door, trying to ignore the thud of tennis balls on the nearby court. Four p.m. The children's dinner was at half-five, then their disco, then the film. Peadar hadn't cancelled the babysitter, but she would need to get out. The prospect of eating in the bedroom, with three children watching her, was unbearable. It would be awkward though, alone in the dining room and then afterwards having to latch onto Joan or somebody else before heading off early to bed.

There was a crunch of gravel. She looked up and spied Chris Conway closing his French door two rooms away. There was only one more room after his. Immediately she knew that it was his footsteps she had heard on the previous two nights. Why? Alison had never known anybody to wander in the gardens after dark. Chris smiled when he saw her and hovered, uncertainly.

'You're enjoying the sun,' he observed.

'When I get the chance.' Alison nodded towards the children inside.

'They'll keep you on your toes all right.' He went to move off, then stopped. It was that old hesitancy, the first time she'd seen it on this holiday. 'Any word of Peadar?'

'No. It's just unfortunate timing.'

'That's true.' He glanced into the room again, then, to her surprise, sat down. 'Listen, Ali, I don't want to ruin your holiday. I can go somewhere else. I hadn't planned on sticking around much longer than the first night anyway.'

'What stopped you?'

He looked away. 'You'd sooner I wasn't here, especially with Peadar gone.'

'No,' she lied.

'It's okay. These last months I've learnt to spot the people I make uncomfortable. It was crazy coming back. I just wanted to see Fitzgerald's again. It's never special unless it's your first time or you know it's your last.'

She remembered sitting on that rock at twelve years old, the magic she had never recaptured.

'You'll come here again,' she said. 'You're young yet.'

'No,' Chris replied. 'I've been in limbo since January, shock, grief. Now I want to say my goodbyes and make a fresh start. You probably think it was strange to come, but I've spent four months running from memories. Eventually there's nowhere left to run.'

'I think you're brave to come.'

Chris openly studied her face, her hair, her figure. It should have felt discomfiting but it wasn't.

'I was never brave, was I?'

Alison looked away. The past should be finished. For Peadar it was, leaving her here with a man who had once loved her as much, if not more, than he did. That was why she had wanted the reassurance of his voice on the phone. She glanced back. Chris looked better now than two decades ago, with more character in his features without the beard. Was she really so unchanged in his eyes or had he made that up?

'You were a coward.' The hurt within her voice surprised her. 'I wasn't some glass ornament, you know.'

He glanced in at the children who were growing restless. 'Would it have made any difference if I'd . . . ?'

'What?'

He shook his head. 'Forget it. I'll be gone by the morning.'

'Don't go,' she said guiltily. 'Not for my sake.'

There were footsteps inside, the click of the television being turned off. Chris rose, allowing his hand to rest on her wrist.

'I'm going for my own sake. But it was so good to see you again.'

His hand lingered for the fraction of a second, bringing back sunshine, a steep winding road in Dalkey between the stone walls of rich gardens. And both of them giddy with laughter as she slid her palm into his, slipping away from the van on their lunch break. How a body feels at eighteen. Intoxicated by life. A sea breeze. Blossom hanging down onto the roadside. Sheila called for her attention as Chris lifted his hand away.

Jack Fitzgerald had obviously spoken to the girls who served the children's dinners, because they seemed aware that Alison was alone and one waitress offered to carry plates for her. Danny attacked his mash and chicken nuggets, but Shane only picked at his food, content to exist on milk. It was hard to get Sheila to eat anything. She was subdued, missing her father. Alison had to repeat things to get her attention.

The first-time mother, Sally, was at her table again, with her husband who looked like he had walked the floor all night. They were leaving tomorrow, the price of five nights being well beyond their reach. Joan came across to rescue her from the attentions of the staff.

'If I'd known you got treated this way I'd have sent Joey home ages ago,' she joked. 'Any word of Peadar?'

'He's probably trying to do ten jobs at once,' Alison replied.

'That sounds like him,' Joan said. 'He's a good man, Peadar. You're lucky. Not all fellows are like that.'

It took twenty seconds of deliberate silence for Alison to realise that Joan was hinting at something.

'What do you mean?'

'If there's one thing I hate it's solitary men lurking around hotels. Who was the guy hassling you in the pool this morning?'

'He wasn't hassling me. We were talking.'

'You weren't the only ones.'

This was crazy. Joan who sat up all night, using language like a docker. Guests mixed here all the time, so why should Alison change her behaviour because Peadar was absent?

'What are you driving at, Joan?'

'Just that Joey wouldn't like me cosying up to somebody as soon as his back was turned.'

The woman was serious, with disapproval in her eyes. Peadar had always found her company boring, the endless impersonations of neighbours on her tiny estate outside Dundalk. 'The only reason Joan sneers at her neighbour's gaudy porch,' Peadar would say, 'is because she can't afford a gaudier one.' Married at seventeen in a dress that didn't fit. 'It was no shotgun wedding,' she'd once joked. 'Joey was in the army. It was a Lee-Enfield.' If things had worked out different, people might still be making jokes about why Alison had married Peadar. It was wrong to look down, but she resented being lectured.

Peadar would laugh if she mentioned Joan's suspicions on the phone, although Alison knew that she wouldn't tell him. She had turned an innocent encounter into something suspicious, but maybe it was just as well Chris was leaving, after the way he'd looked at her for a second this afternoon. Joan made some girlie remark, realising her advice was unwanted. But Alison knew she would spend this holiday avoiding Joan. They had nothing in common, except the coincidence of staying here. Shane pulled at her sleeve, asking for an ice cream. He would only take one bite of the cone, but Alison was glad of the excuse to escape. She walked away, with Joan telling her to join them for a drink that evening.

———————

Her words to Danny about being in charge must have played on his mind, because when the human train was being formed to go to the video room, Danny insisted she have a rest and let him mind the family. She smiled, watching him usher Shane and Sheila into line, his manner unconsciously impersonating Peadar's. They marched off, with Sheila looking back a little uncertainly.

Alison had been expecting a phone call and twice checked at reception for any messages she might have missed. She phoned home again but got the answering machine. The blips told her there were seventeen messages on the tape, eleven more than earlier. The school phone kept ringing and she refused to try McCann's home number. There were a half dozen meetings that Peadar could be attending or maybe he was grabbing a bite to eat. She wished she wasn't so susceptible to suggestion, but Joan's remark had left a sour taste.

In ten minutes she would check the children, but now she went out into the gardens. For once the crazy golf course was empty, with just a few older couples on the patio, doing crosswords or sitting in companionable silence.

The upper storey of the Slaney Room led out onto an open-air balcony. Chris Conway leaned on the rail there, watching the ferry depart the distant harbour.

Alison might never have joined him were it not for Joan's words. But she needed to assert her independence, even though nobody was watching. It was hot when she entered the Slaney Room and she was glad to ascend the curving staircase to the upper level and push the glass doors open. Chris was alone on the balcony.

'What news from the front?' he asked.

'The children are quartered before a video.'

'Long may the peace last.' He turned back to watch the ferry. What direction was he going in afterwards, she wondered? France, Germany, Spain? How far had you to travel to start a new life? Even if you couldn't understand one word the local children said, surely they would still remind you in a hundred ways. Alison rested her elbow on the rail beside his and looked out across the grounds. Part of her wanted Joan to appear and glance up disapprovingly.

'Any word from Peadar?'

'He's probably eating out. It's hardly much fun going home to an empty house.'

'No.' There was no intonation in his voice, but she regretted the remark.

'That must have been hard,' she said tentatively. 'After the funeral, going back to an empty house.'

'It wasn't empty.' He looked at her. 'That was the problem. I couldn't get rid of hordes of well-meaning people with nothing useful to say.'

The remark hurt, though she couldn't be sure if there was a barb in it. She sensed now that Chris couldn't wait to be gone.

'Where will you go tomorrow?'

'Somewhere different.' Another couple came out onto the balcony, watching the ferry turn in a giant loop before heading for France. Chris seemed uncomfortable with her. She should leave him alone, yet how long was it since she'd had this effect on any man? Her own husband rushing off to do business sooner than spend time with her. How many other women had there been in Chris's life?

There were terribly intimate questions she wanted to ask this man who had once offered to marry her, clumsily at a Christmas party, long after the whole office became aware that she was pregnant with Peadar's child. He had got drunk and locked them into the bathroom of a Rathmines flat while the ceiling shook with dancing feet. Even then Chris had been obsequious, caging his offer in terms of things not working out between Peader and herself, casting himself in the role of fall-guy. 'That's sweet of you, Chris,' she'd replied, taking his hand as if to calm a nervous child. Later, when leaving, she had seen him collapsed in a corner and placed a coat over his shoulder. That was the weekend she miscarried and the last time she had seen him before this holiday.

The Irwins emerged below, Mr Irwin stooping to collect two putters off the grass. They walked companionably towards the first hole. Alison hoped they wouldn't look up, even though it was ridiculous to think she was doing anything wrong. She was a happily married woman, or as happily married as any woman her age was if you spoke honestly to them. Besides Chris seemed locked inside a pain now which she could barely even fathom.

'Peadar would have liked to have had a drink with you,' she said.

'Yeah.' He nodded. 'I always admired Peadar.'

She couldn't detect irony in his voice. His hand brushed against hers but this time he was pointing. Sheila stood on the grass below, near tears, looking around for her. Alison called and the child started running.

Sheila was struggling with the doors of the Slaney Room by the time Alison reached her and gathered her daughter up in her arms.

'I didn't like the dinosaurs in the film, Mammy,' she sobbed. 'They gave me a headache.'

'What do you mean?'

'Like my head is too heavy.'

Sheila should have worn a sunhat this afternoon. Lotion wasn't enough to protect her. The child's face looked puffy and tired. The sun came out through clouds and Sheila raised a hand to shield her eyes from it.

'I want to go to bed,' she said. 'I want Daddy.'

Alison soothed her as she began to cry. She looked back at the balcony, but Chris Conway was gone.

———— ❧ ————

Of all the children Sheila had the most sensitive skin. Alison had taken a risk in using perfumed shower gel on her after their morning swim and by bedtime the child's tummy was covered in a light heat rash. She was cranky and exhausted, asking for her father. Alison even phoned home again, convinced that Peadar would be there by now and could at least speak to the girl. The blip count of 'messages received' was up to twenty-four. She didn't leave a message but suspected the answering machine memory was probably full at this stage.

She might not have gone down for dinner if the babysitter hadn't bustled her out, explaining that her hovering around was only making Sheila worse. Alison made the woman promise to page her if the child didn't settle, then stood outside the door listening until Sheila stopped crying as the woman read her a story.

She had never eaten dinner alone in a crowded room before. It was hard not to feel that people were watching from the moment she entered. Even the couples nearby seemed to lower their voices as if suspicious of her eavesdropping. She regretted not bringing a book, but knew that she lacked the panache to casually read through her meal.

The long dining room was filled with a hubbub of

chatter. Evening dress was requested and young children frowned on after seven o'clock but it always surprised her to see the few casually-dressed younger couples who brought children in. She chose roast stuffed saddle of lamb Dauphinoise with gratin of potato. It was Peadar's favourite meal, with finely chopped shallots and rosemary in the stuffing. Where was he now? Judging by the answering machine a lot of people were after him or the same people very badly. Yet she resented his silence, when he could have phoned from somewhere.

The lamb was perfectly cooked, its familiar taste adding to his absence. Across the room the Bennetts nodded as they rose after their meal. Mr BMW was complaining to a waiter – about life in general, she suspected – while his daughters practised pouting. He would probably only be satisfied with a written apology from God. Two tables away an elderly couple held hands with their food barely touched. The man wore a bow tie at least thirty years old. His wife's eyes were bird-bright, shining. How lucky they were, Alison thought, to still have, and enjoy, each other's company.

Joan was trying to attract her eye. It was foolish to pro-long a quarrel with somebody you barely knew, but Alison avoided looking back. She wanted to be alone. What if Joan had glimpsed some unconscious temptation within her this morning? Had she been flaunting herself slightly, flattered by Chris's attention, by any attention? She dismissed the idea, but then why had he suddenly chosen to leave? Ironically, it was the very absence of anything physical between herself and Chris which made their relationship seem so special with time. Through Peadar's eyes she could see herself screaming in labour-pangs or haggard from sleeplessness when a child was sick.

Knowing crises of inner despair as she sensed her body ageing. Years of kitchens crammed with dishes, piles of clothes for ironing. Voices complaining on the radio, supermarket queues, meaningless talk in mother and toddler groups. Peadar had been there at every stage, seeing her differently at different times. The way he never found her as tight after the stitches following her caesarean section with Sheila. How she could walk through the bedroom naked now after a shower and he would no longer automatically put a hand out to fondle her.

Chris still seemed to see the eighteen-year-old girl preserved inside this thirty-eight-year-old woman, saw her with no complications in between. The thought was frightening. Surely he must see the wrinkles and changes, the slight sag of her breasts. Perhaps only he could be the true judge of how her body had withstood two decades of living. Yet his eyes seemed non-judgemental. Maybe it was vanity to think he still cared.

She knew little about his life since that Monday morning when she started to miscarry, climbing down from a mobile van in Santry, and never returned to work afterwards. He had been working an afternoon shift, not there when it happened.

What had his wife been like? Were they happy together? Somehow Alison had imagined him staying single, never having found – she knew this was adolescent conceit – the right replacement for her. Would he find someone again now?

She wondered if Peadar ever wished them all gone from around his neck, in those black moods when he pretended to work in his room upstairs? Surely there were times when everyone fantasised about having a fresh start, but never like this. Alison had noticed how tender she was with her children all day, finding excuses to touch them, brush back their hair, hug and plant kisses on their necks, as if storing memories up. She could imagine no other life than her present one and the purposelessness of the years to come, when they would move naturally away from her, was something she already dreaded.

Alison was thankful that Jack Fitzgerald wasn't on duty tonight. She didn't feel like small talk. Her hot walnut pudding arrived with ice cream. She ordered coffee, wishing for once that she hadn't stopped smoking when pregnant with Danny. Smokers always looked self-contained at a table, engaged in doing something. Had Jane smoked? Plain Jane? Jane the sophisticate? Alison imagined a woman with blonde hair tied up, laughing at a table like this, confident and knowing. Every time the door opened she expected a waiter to beckon her to a phone. Nine-fifty. Surely Peadar was home by now, though knowing him he would be too concerned about waking the kids – especially Danny with his night terrors – to phone the room this late.

She decided to phone him and left her dessert unfinished. A log fire blazed in the reading room. The elderly couple she had seen holding hands at dinner sat in silence on two armchairs there, beyond the need of words.

The payphone was located in an alcove. The answering machine came on again, but the succession of blips was cleared. Peadar had been in and gone out again, or else he was there now, bizarrely listening to her leaving a message. Why would she even think such a thing? Still Alison waited a moment after she finished talking, hoping he might pick up the receiver. She could imagine her own sitting room, with her voice having startled the shadows there. Then she put the phone down.

She was concerned about Sheila, but knew she would

only disturb Danny by returning this early. Alison decided to parole herself until ten-thirty. The glass doors out onto the roadway were open. She stood in the porch, staring across at the car park through the heavy rain that had threatened all evening. The battered van parked incongruously among the sleek cars must belong to Chris. Alison would never again think their own car out of place among the grander models there. The narrow road, leading to guesthouses and B&Bs and then the wind-swept golfing links, was deserted. The noise of the rain was soothing. She didn't want to face the crowded Slaney Room, yet couldn't stay out here.

Sally's husband ran in from the car park carrying a baby-changing bag. He nodded, shaking rain from his jacket. Seamus, the night porter, was on duty. Alison sensed him hover behind her, concerned she might want some message done. She went back in, smiling to him.

The Slaney Room was packed. Joan and Joey were planked with two other couples at a table beside the dance floor. She slipped upstairs to the upper tier before they saw her. It was less crowded here, mainly with couples who did not intend dancing. At a small table, gazing down, Chris Conway sat alone. It was the table she would have picked, on the edge of things yet out of sight. He was nursing an Irish Mist, with two empty glasses on the table beside him.

Perhaps he was waiting in hope for her, his jacket on the other chair as if reserving it. But she chose the only other free table, right at the back where she could watch him, and ordered a rum and coke from a passing waiter.

From there, Alison could see half the dance floor but only the legs of the band. Joey's bald patch was in view, but she only glimpsed Joan whenever the woman leaned forward for her drink. It was a different perspective. If Peadar was still with her they would be down there now, roped into that group who stopped talking to join in the applause as two tango performers came out to present their weekly display.

This was new, but she only half watched the dancers begin their routine. Instead, feeling like a voyeur, she observed Chris Conway watching them. The fringe of his hair was grey. She hadn't noticed that before. She wondered about his present life, with all that free time which wasn't consumed by the demands of children. Time not crammed into a schedule of school runs, art classes and swimming lessons. Time as it had once stretched out when she was a schoolgirl lying in bed on Saturday mornings or, later on, sharing that flat on Beechwood Avenue with two other trainee nurses.

She could still recall evenings there, with voices from the greengrocer's across the road wafting through the bay window as Carmel boiled up Kerr's Pinks or Queens potatoes – 'great balls of flour', as she called them – while grilling the cheapest pork chops. None of them ever seemed to have a penny from Monday to Thursday. They sat in or visited other flats, watching TV, talking, planning dances or weekend drinking parties, discussing men disparagingly, laughing about the hospital matron and putting their futures on hold.

The only thing they had owned in that flat was time. Whole evenings spent talking and smoking. Nights when they would troop out for cigarettes at two a.m., Carmel or Susan waking her up by calling across the shared bedroom to say they were dying for a drag.

New kebab shops were opening along Rathmines Road

that year, with late-night traffic pulsing past towards Rathgar and Terenure. They would sit on the bench opposite the twenty-four-hour store to light up, enjoying the night air and laughing at their own craziness, when they knew they had an early shift to start in a few hours' time.

Alison had never told the others that she'd been pregnant. It had seemed like a bad dream, something to be airbrushed from her life. If she had been able to look into the future, then surely she would be pleased to find herself here. All her dreams, or at least her safest ones, come through. Yet she knew that the twenty-year-old smoking on a bench in Rathmines would view her present incarnation as a stranger, burdened down and cheated by time.

The tango display continued. Alison could see girls from the kitchen crowding a doorway to glimpse the whirling figures. Girls overworked and probably underpaid, but still with the gift of time. The kitchen staff nudged each other and laughed as the man threw his partner flamboyantly over his shoulder. The local band played on, glad to be released from their normal medley of musical standards. This display was still novel, but within another few months the girls wouldn't bother sneaking away from their pots and pans. It would blend into the seamless routine of each identical week, which was the mainstay of Fitzgerald's.

The same menus, same songs, the same medals for kids after the magic show every Thursday. The same couples choosing the same week every year. If his family had not been killed, Alison and Chris could have continued coming here all their lives without ever meeting like this. He turned suddenly, as if looking for her, and pointed upwards. She was confused, then

realised he was drawing her attention to a muffled announcement, which came again, asking for her to return to her room.

Alison rose, startled, and descended the stairs, almost
running along the corridor. The door was ajar, the light on
in the bathroom. There was vomit on the tiles and Sheila
knelt, groggily, with her head over the toilet bowl. The babysitter looked up from beside her. Alison knew the woman was
worried. She tried not to panic.

'I don't mind the vomiting,' the babysitter said, 'but I
can't seem to really get her attention.'

Alison knelt, turning the child around to face her. Sheila
screwed up her eyes as if the light hurt. Alison pulled up her
pyjama top. The rash was far worse now, with blotches on
her chest and arms.

'My head hurts,' the child mumbled, 'my head.'

'Look down at your toes,' Alison commanded, her tone
sharpened with fear.

'I don't want to.'

'It may just be too much sun.' The babysitter tried to
calm her. 'Sometimes it affects children and then the holiday
excitement gets too much for them.'

'Look up at the light, then down at your toes. Please,
pet, please,' Alison begged.

The child seemed unable or unwilling to. She looked
dazed, with barely enough strength to stand. She sank to her
knees before the toilet and retched, although nothing was left
in her stomach. Alison became aware of Chris Conway in the
open doorway.

'I just wanted to make sure everything was all right,' he
said.

'Her neck is stiff. She has a headache and rash and can't seem to stand bright lights.'

She didn't have to mention the word. All three were thinking of meningitis. It was two weeks since Sheila's class was notified that Jean O'Connor had it, with her grandmother driving her to the hospital just in time. The incubation period could be weeks.

'I'll phone reception,' the babysitter said. 'They can call a doctor.'

'There isn't time.' Alison looked at Chris. 'Can you drive me to Wexford hospital?'

'I don't know.' He hesitated. 'I've had a few drinks.'

'This is an emergency,' she argued. 'Peadar drives with a few drinks.'

'I'm not Peadar,' Chris replied defensively.

'You never were.' The barb was cruel, but she was frantic with worry. She couldn't wait for the night porter to arrange a lift. She had to be gone now, holding her child, doing something. Every second counted with the possibility of meningitis.

'Can you mind the boys?' Chris was addressing the babysitter. She nodded and he took out his car keys from his pocket. The babysitter told her that Peadar had phoned twice, before Sheila started to stir. She had passed him back to the switchboard but if an announcement was made Alison had never heard it.

Alison wrapped Sheila in a blanket, kissing the whimpering child. It felt unreal, like a nightmare. The night porter was startled to see them run down the corridor. He followed them out to the van, trying to help. If it was meningitis then the boys could be brewing it too. Her precious children. The gears grinded as Chris edged between the pillars. In the rain, his wipers could hardly keep the windscreen clear. The road was empty but he seemed to drive unnaturally slow, chugging cautiously over the hump-backed bridge and heading for the main road.

She stared across impatiently, willing him on. He seemed oblivious to her, peeping out at ditches flashing past in the headlights. Fifty miles an hour without another car in sight. Surely to God he could go faster than that?

'Come on, Chris,' she hissed. 'Do you want us to get there at all?'

She could sense the child's fear on her knee. Sheila seemed disorientated, with a rocketing temperature. The speedometer flickered to fifty-five then dropped back again. The road was half flooded in shallows, the rain incessant now. Alison realised she didn't even know where the bloody hospital was in Wexford.

'Come on, a bit faster,' she snapped, 'for God's sake.'

'Just shut the fuck up!' Chris's voice startled her, not in its anger but its fear. She noticed he was sweating. 'Maybe Peadar is Superman, but Peadar isn't bloody here, is he? I'll get the child there safely, that's what counts.'

In her anxiety she hadn't thought about the crash. How hard was it for him to drive at night with a child? What demons was he confronting?

'I'm sorry,' he muttered, quietly.

'No, I'm sorry.'

'How is she doing?'

'Burning up.'

'She'll be all right.'

'How do you know?'

'Sara had septicaemia when she was three. The worst night of my life.' Chris paused. 'The second worst. Her skin was different than this, far worse.' He looked across. 'Still I could be wrong. Never take chances with a child.'

Alison gazed down at her daughter who seemed to be drifting towards sleep. It was impossible to conceive of life without her. Even the thought conjured up an arid infinity of pain.

'How do you cope?' she asked. 'I mean, what do you do?'

They had reached the main road. A truck zoomed past with twinkling lights. Chris swung right, staring out into the rain.

'These last months I've played a lot of golf mainly.'

Golf. She felt let down and almost angry. How masculine could you get? Your wife and children die, so you console yourself by golfing with your pals. Yet it was probably what Peadar would do. She could imagine Peadar in the clubhouse in Donabate, men clustered around him, careful of what they said. Lifts would be arranged when he drank too much, four-balls organised, his gimme range extended by six inches. In time there would be dinner invitations, discreet potential dates lined up.

Alison knew she was being bitchy, feeling abandoned. Peadar would be devastated without her. No friends could compensate for knowing in your heart that you were utterly alone. Yet Peadar could survive such a tragedy, whereas she would go to pieces, locked up or dead within months.

'It's good that you've golf to enjoy.' She tried not to make it sound like a putdown.

'I don't enjoy it. I don't enjoy anything.'

Chris managed to increase his speed on the main road, but she could see how much of a strain the driving was. How many drinks had he got through, and had the driver who'd killed his family been drinking too?

'Why do you play then?'

Chris shrugged. 'There's enough space to be left alone on most courses, if you set out early. I gave my car away and kept this van that we used for deliveries. I fitted out the back of it, put in a bed, a gas stove, pots, pans. It's all right, just a bit cold at night.'

'You mean you've been living in it?'

'I drive home occasionally. It's crazy, a phobia. I get out, stand on the lawn. I don't know what I'm afraid to find inside but each time I just get back into this van and drive off again.'

'Your house could be robbed,' she said. 'Thieves cruise around, notice everything.'

'What's left to rob? Nothing I want anyway.'

There was no self-pity in the voice. A truck sped past, with a car trying to overtake it, forcing Chris onto the hard shoulder. If there was a checkpoint she knew that he would lose his licence because of her.

'It's up for sale now,' he added. 'The girls' clothes went to charity shops.'

'You're keeping nothing?'

'My partner even got the dog.'

'And you just play golf?'

'Some clubs get shirty about the van being parked overnight, not that they know there's somebody sleeping inside. But you need a structure to your day. Up at dawn, brew some tea, then out. More often than not I just leave money in an envelope in a box.'

'Do you not get tired of it?' she asked.

'Some mornings I can hardly hold the bloody driver, let alone care where the ball goes. Just hit the blasted thing and walk on, cursing myself every time it flies into the rough. Maybe you feel wrecked, but at least you feel something. Eighteen holes, then lunch, then another eighteen if there's no outing on the course. Ending up in the bloody dusk. Then on to another club car park, a few drinks at the bar and I'm so wrecked I fall asleep before the barman locking up starts wondering who left their van behind.'

'That's no way to live,' she said.

'It's a way to keep living, keep moving. I actually got a hole-in-one. Last Tuesday. The seventeenth at Seapoint near Baltray. Teeing off up on dunes with the Irish Sea below and the Mourne Mountains covered in cloud across Carlingford Bay. A gale blowing, rain and spray in my face. I hit a low four iron, one hundred and sixty-four metres. No fairway or anything, just the green peeking through a gap in the dunes with a rabbit path winding towards it. It bounced once, four feet from the pin, then ran in.'

Chris shook his head ruefully and laughed.

'A hundred and sixty-four metres in the teeth of wind and rain. The shot of a lifetime. And just me there. Nobody else on the bloody course. Not even a gull overhead to yell at.'

'How did you feel?' she asked, stroking her daughter's hair, trying to keep talking and not to panic.

'Deflated,' he replied, 'in shock. God knows how long it was since I'd had a proper meal or slept in a bed. The green-keeper was leaving trolleys out. He didn't even know I'd been on the course. I could have told him, but I didn't. It was my secret. I wanted to throw the clubs away. It was finished, I was going home. I was telling nobody until I told Jane.'

He went silent, carefully negotiating the roundabout before Wexford town. Jane Conway. Sara Conway. Rachel Conway. How could she have missed such a trinity of deaths in the *Irish Times*? Though it was at the time when Dr O'Gorman had sent her for the mammogram, when she was pre-occupied with her own concerns. '*Deeply regretted by her loving husband, Chris.*' Surely his name would have stood out for her.

'Do you often forget she's dead?'

'I did last Tuesday,' he replied. 'For a whole ten seconds. The time it took to start the van, then remember that I'd nothing to go home to. You don't forget people are dead, it's just that sometimes you forget their death is forever.'

Sheila stirred and made a retching noise. She looked up, scared, uncertain where she was.

'Don't worry,' Chris said. 'It's not what you think. I know. I know. I know.'

He made it sound like a mantra, used to cover up his own fear. He repeated it again, jarring on her nerves.

'You don't know,' she snapped, succumbing to panic again. 'This is my daughter we're talking about.'

123

The hospital was on a hill overlooking Wexford. The casualty department quiet before the pubs emptied. Alison rushed her in, with Chris lagging behind. Sheila was more distressed now, scared by the noise and lights and sensing the fear that her mother tried to disguise.

Once Alison mentioned the meningitis scare at Sheila's school the nurses showed her into a cubicle. Chris stayed back but Alison waved him in. She was shaking and needed somebody beside her. The doctor was African with an impenetrable accent. He seemed to take forever, rechecking the child's temperature, shining lights in her eyes, manipulating her neck. Alison's years of nursing were of no benefit when it came to being a patient's mother. The anxiety was worse for her memories of seeing other children suffer. Chris found her hand, squeezing it so tight his grip hurt. But she was glad of the comfort and squeezed back, almost afraid to let go.

'You the father?' the doctor asked Chris.

'No.' Chris seemed equally nervous. God knows what sights he had last confronted in a room like this.

'Do you want to go?' she asked.

'No.' His voice was grim, his fingers almost crushing hers.

The doctor made Sheila open her mouth again, using a wooden spatula to hold down her tongue. The child cried with fright, causing him to have to start again. He looked up eventually.

'Tonsillitis,' he said. 'Her throat is raw, causing headache. Ponston now for the pain, then antibiotics.'

'But the rash . . .' Alison began.

'An allergy. She eat something different?'

The perfumed shower gel on Sheila's skin. Alison closed

her eyes, thanking God. Previously she had been too scared to even pray.

'And no sign of septicaemia or meningitis?' she asked.

'Look.' The doctor pressed a small glass against the spots on Sheila's tummy. They faded under the pressure. 'If they did not fade, you would need to go to a hospital immediately.'

'But she was right to come and take no chances,' Chris said, as if defending her. He let go her hand. Alison wanted to put her arms around him in relief, yet she felt stupid at the same time. She was a trained nurse. These were basic things she should have checked instead of panicking.

'She was right,' the doctor agreed. 'Last year I saw a boy die. His parents left it too late, not wanting to waste hospital time.' He looked closely at Chris. 'Have you been drinking?'

'I drove us here,' Alison said quickly. The doctor ruffled Sheila's hair and moved off as a nurse brought the painkiller and antibiotic. Sheila was cranky, her throat sore. It took so long to persuade her to swallow the medicine that it was ten minutes before Alison noticed Chris was missing.

She left Sheila with the nurse. There was no sign of him in casualty or at the van. It was on the way back in that she saw him outside on a bench. He held his head in his hands and she knew that he was crying. She sat beside him, awkwardly, unsure what to do.

'It's okay,' she said.

'It's not okay. It will never be okay.'

'Is there anything I can do?'

'I'll drive you back. Tomorrow I'll be gone.'

'You don't have to go.' Alison was trembling now, almost giddy with relief that Sheila was okay.

'I do.'

'Why?' she asked.

'Because you're the last bloody person I want to meet just now.'

He lifted his head, looking straight at her. It happened because she wanted to comfort him or because she was drunk with relief or from some impulse she didn't understand. She didn't even know who moved their head first, just that suddenly the temptation was there. For the shock of one single moment she had her arms around his neck and they kissed. Just like that previous kiss had occurred in Dalkey, the steep road, high stone walls, blossoms hanging down. Except this wasn't the same. It was twenty years later. She drew her head back, alarmed and confused.

'Can't you see?' Chris said. 'You complicate everything, Ali. You're about the only living person I still care for.'

———— ❧ ————

Sheila was like a different child after the Ponston, sitting up and playing with toys the nurses had found, when Alison went back in. The girl was almost light-headed in the van, savouring her adventure but, by the time they reached the roundabout, she had fallen asleep again. The silence in the van was awkward, with neither of them seeming to know what to say.

'Chris . . . I . . .' Alison hesitated.

'I know. Forget it happened. It was my fault.'

Alison stared ahead, sensing the tension between them.

'Does anyone know you're down here?'

'Who's left to know?'

'Family. Friends. You do have friends, don't you?'

'Don't worry,' Chris said. 'I didn't become some mad loner. I had a life of stunning ordinariness. So many friends it took hours after the funeral to get rid of everyone. Plates of food, women washing up, men pouring drinks. Some poor neighbour asking me, "Where does Jane keep her wine glasses?" then going white with embarrassment.

'It was one a.m. before I saw off my partner who looked like he wanted to remove my shoelaces or anything else I might hang myself with. That only left me and the blasted dog. I'd never liked him anyway, I only got him for the girls who ignored him once the novelty wore off. There he was whining, staring up at his lead. He didn't care who was dead, he just wanted his walk. Big beseeching eyes. I wanted to throw him into the river but out I went and walked the blasted legs off him.'

The rain had stopped now, a crescent moon lighting the empty road. Chris seemed unable to stop talking, frightened of what silence might bring.

'The poor dog didn't know what was happening. He strained at his lead for the first mile, then started looking up, waiting to turn for home. But I kept going, through the toughest parts of Ballybough and down the seafront at Clontarf. Rain bucketing down, no one around, just two stray lovers in a concrete shelter and some winos in another. The dog's tail was down, his breath in pants. I wanted to get soaked, I wanted phenomena. I wanted to fling myself onto the rocks below. Hardly a car passing except for taxis ploughing through the puddles. Pubs in darkness, shops bolted up. We reached the wooden bridge onto Bull Island. I took his lead off, shoving him on ahead with my foot when he refused to budge.'

Chris shook his head, as though amused by the memory.

'I swear to Christ, Ali, even the dog was trying to mind me. He only stopped short of putting a paw out to hail a passing taxi. I walked through the dark towards the bridge. He stayed at the traffic lights, whining. They say dogs can sense danger. I could hear night birds call across the mudflats. Then I heard his paws on the wooden sleepers at my heel. That crazy dog. God knows who might be out there, sleeping rough, shooting up. I'd be a soft touch with a wad of notes in my wallet. They were welcome to try and rob it, but I'd fight to the end. That was the point. I wanted an end to everything. I'd have welcomed some joyrider crossing that bridge, not seeing me till I stepped into his headlights and got killed.'

'You didn't really want that,' Alison said, uneasily. The van had picked up speed. He was doing sixty-five now, seventy. His hands were trembling, his eyes slightly glazed. Just how many drinks did he have back in the hotel? She looked down at Sheila, knowing how irresponsible she had been in forcing him to drive.

'I don't know what I wanted,' he replied. 'Maybe just to feel something again. I wanted their ghosts to haunt me. A hundred times we'd walked across that bridge, the girls taking turns to hold the dog's lead. I wanted to feel close to them, but it didn't work. The dead are dead and that's it. I reached the Bull Wall, built right out into the sea. No one around. The bloody dog had miles of sand dunes to his left. Do you think he'd run off? He stuck to my heels with his tail down. I walked across the crumbling stones, out and out with the sea wild on both sides of me.

'There were some old concrete bathing shelters. I stepped into each one, looking for my killer. I virtually waved my wallet in the air. The bloody dog circling my heels. I fell over him twice. The second time I picked him up. I couldn't bear the thought of him day after day, wanting to be walked, fed and minded. That was the cruellest joke, he was all I'd left of my family. Years of working for our future and the only responsibility I had left was a dog I'd never even liked.'

'You didn't kill him.' The van's speed frightened her, the way Chris stared out at the road.

'I hadn't got it in me. Three times I went to throw him onto the rocks.' Chris slowed the van and looked over. 'I was always a coward, remember.'

'I remember you as gentle.'

'Gentleness never got me far.' There was enough regret in his tone for her to experience an unanticipated sensation of goosebumps. 'If I'd killed him that night I'd have killed myself too. Nothing to stop me, no messy loose ends. Stupid bloody dog. I found a bar of Sara's favourite chocolate in my pocket. I fed it to him, then blacked out in a shelter with him curled at my feet. I woke at dawn. I've never known such coldness. A tramp stood over me, his face blue. "Get away to hell," he said. "You don't belong." The dog was shivering, that beseeching look. I got a taxi on the coast road and stopped to buy food for him.'

The left turn came for Rosslare. It was half-one, the road here still flooded. She wondered how much she should pay the babysitter or whether Danny might have woken. She worried about every kind of mundane thing to try and block other thoughts out. She was a happily married woman. Chris was a widower. It didn't matter what her body told her. She crushed the nerve ends of her fingers so tightly together that her nails turned white. Tomorrow she would resume her normal life and he would be gone. It was Peadar's fault for leaving her stranded here without a car. The child slept on her knee, her flesh less hot. She blocked out the feel of Chris's skin, the memory of the warmth of his hand.

'Did you love her?' Alison shocked herself with the remark.

'What type of question is that?'

'You don't have to answer.'

'Do you love Peadar? Still?'

The isolated garage where they got petrol every year was closed. Chris passed it, turning left.

'Yes. But I've loved him differently at different times.'

'Of course I loved Jane,' Chris said. 'You don't share what we shared unless you love someone. But it's . . .'

He turned right, the van slowing. She thought he was going to stop. The back was rigged out, with a bed, a stove. Surely he knew she didn't want that. She couldn't afford to want anything. Her life was fixed, set out. He drove carefully, searching for words.

'It's not as simple as when you're young,' he went on. 'I shared things with Jane. We were equals, no pedestals. What are you asking? Did she consume me like a knot in my throat? Was she the first thing I thought of when I woke? The last thing I saw at night? A flame burning me even when out of reach?'

'Chris . . . ?' His intensity frightened her.

'First love is different. It's not tested by tedium or middle age.'

'I shouldn't have asked the question.'

'I asked it myself often enough these last months,' he said. 'I bought her a car for Christmas, a Honda Accord, two years old, eleven thousand on the clock. Jane didn't want so big a car, but I saw a hand-written ad with a local phone number in a shop window. Three thousand quid less than a garage would charge. A bargain, you understand?'

They crossed the hump-backed bridge, with the sea dark before them.

'You'd think I'd understand greed in my trade. The guy who answered the phone baaed like a sheep. Except the car belonged to his cousin, a Sam Burns in Leitrim. The Kerry numberplates gave me the first hint something was wrong, that and Burns' Belfast accent when he drove it up. A Belfastman based in Leitrim, selling a Kerry registered car in Dublin. The bodywork was pristine bodywork, the engine a dream. It was his wife's, he said, but she was leaving her job because she was pregnant. Burns didn't look a man to give something away cheap. Only one owner on the logbook and it wasn't him. He hadn't entered his name so as not to bring the value down. I wanted to ask if he was a dealer, had it been crashed, but if Jane heard such talk she'd have never touched the car. And it was a bargain. My mechanic could find nothing wrong, but at that price he said he wouldn't touch it. Burns kept calling, saying other buyers were interested. Jane got suspicious when I couldn't make up my mind. But three grand saved was three grand and there was nothing wrong with the bloody car.'

'So what was the problem?' Alison asked.

'With first love there's no balancing the books.' Chris looked at her with neither guile nor shyness. 'I'd never have taken the risk with you. I'd have spent every penny on the latest model.'

He drove into the car park and switched the engine off. They sat in silence.

'Peadar would have bought me the car you got Jane,' she said quietly.

'They died in that car. The police say it was the other driver's fault. He skidded across the road.'

'If that's what the police say . . .'

'Maybe they're wrong. Maybe the brakes or the steering . . . maybe something snapped when she tried to swerve out of his way.'

'You can't blame yourself.'

His voice was harsh. 'Is there somebody else left to blame?'

'Chris . . .' She wanted to touch his hand that still gripped the wheel. 'Back at the hospital . . . I was just so happy Sheila was safe.'

'I know.'

'But finish your holiday. Don't disappear.'

'You don't understand, Ali.'

'I understand it won't happen again. Thank you for driving us.'

132

Jack Fitzgerald was waiting in reception. He had phoned the hospital and got the news already. One minute Chris was behind her, the next he had vanished.

They spoke in whispers so as not to wake the child, Jack accompanying her up the corridor. The babysitter looked so relieved she was almost in tears. She refused to take extra money and disappeared, leaving Alison alone.

She should phone Peadar now, keeping her voice low, but she felt drained, unable to talk. Alison undressed, pulled back the sheets and then stopped. She put a dressing gown on and crossed to the window, pulling the drapes closed behind her. She stood, concealed between the drapes and long net curtains. Parts of the gardens were lit by lamps concealed in trees, but whole sections lay in darkness. The sky had grown black with more rain clouds, the roar of waves almost lost behind the double-glazing.

Her child was safe, life went on. She needed sleep to face tomorrow. But she wanted to see if Chris would surreptitiously cross the gravel again, inches from her but not knowing she was there. Alison waited till she couldn't stand up any more with tiredness, confused and disturbed by this need to watch over him if he passed in the tight vice-grip of his pain.

# WEDNESDAY

In her dream Alison was thirty-eight, yet somehow also eighteen again. Lying in her old bedroom in Waterford, forced to study for exams she thought she had completed years ago. She didn't know what made her call out, just that she suddenly woke. The room in Fitzgerald's was dark and Danny stood over her bed.

'You cried out,' he whispered. 'You cried for Daddy.'

Danny walked back to his bed. She lay awake, confused and disorientated, then rose to check that Sheila was okay. She knew she had cried out, not for Peadar but for her own father, as if she herself were a child again.

———— ✥ ————

Peadar phoned at eight-thirty, just when Alison was finished giving Sheila her antibiotic. Once she'd been given Calpol for her throat, Sheila was in high spirits, boasting to the disbelieving boys about her trip into Wexford. Danny and Shane already had the door open to march down to breakfast. Alison called the boys back, forcing them to sit on the bed, but they were hungry and impatient. They had been up since half-seven, playing around while she took Sheila into her bed and tried to snatch a few extra moments of sleep. She knew they could not be corralled for much longer.

Besides, she didn't know what to say to Peadar about

last night. The scare with Sheila seemed almost secondary now. But there was nothing illicit in taking a lift from Chris. He had helped out when Peadar was off God knows where. Their kiss was one of relief that the child was well.

Yet her face was hot and she cursed herself for blushing like she hadn't blushed in years. Danny watched her with an echo of the look Peadar sometimes had. She turned away from the child.

'If I can get this liquidator officially appointed I could leave the rest to McCann and get back down,' Peadar was saying. 'As it is, there are so many suppliers swarming over the site that it's like a car boot sale.'

Peadar was Sheila's father, she had to tell him about the hospital visit. But she didn't want him rushing back just for his daughter. Alison wanted him here for her sake, to know that she counted for something too.

She knew Sheila was dying to tell her father about it, but she waved the child away. There were daggers in Danny's eyes as he pulled impatient faces.

'I need you to be here with me,' she said.

'I want to be there too. I miss you.' His voice sounded plaintive, then changed in the way it did when McCann or someone entered his office. Yet until then she had presumed he was phoning from home. Why was he at the school so early? 'I'll phone later,' he said, more business-like.

'Where are you calling from?' she asked.

'Dublin.' He laughed. 'You silly goose.'

Danny wrenched the phone from her hands. 'We love you, we miss you, we're absolutely starving. Goodbye,' he said in a rush, while the youngest two laughed. 'That's nice.'

He hung on long enough to listen to something Peadar said. 'I made it especially shiny.' He replaced the receiver and turned to her. 'Now breakfast.'

'That's not clever, it's rude,' she hissed. 'I hadn't finished what I wanted to tell Daddy.'

The boy threw his eyes to heaven. 'You're never finished anything,' he shouted back. 'I'm parched. I need a drink of milk or I'll go crazy. I wish Daddy was here. He'd have been up hours ago. He'd have us in the pool by now.'

Alison knew that behind his toughness he was seconds away from tears. She put an arm around him and steered him out the door, resisting the urge to brush his hair that was sticking up again.

'Breakfast in a flash,' she said, 'and I'll have you in the pool in no time.'

The others ran ahead but he stayed beside her. She looked down, knowing him too well.

'When's Daddy coming back?' he asked.

'As soon as he possibly can.'

'You go swimming. I'll play around the garden.'

Alison was shocked. Even at six months old he had loved the water. Normally he would spend all day in the pool if allowed to.

'Of course you want to go swimming.'

'I'll play with the twins,' he replied stubbornly. 'We have our own club.'

'To hell with your bloody club,' she hissed angrily, as they entered the sunlit foyer. 'Your family are more important than some bloody club. Just because you make a few friends doesn't mean you suddenly forget the rest of us.'

Tears appeared below the surface of his eyes. She was annoyed with herself for snapping and being so rattled this morning. Children grow up and away from you. It was just that on this holiday she seemed to keep losing bits of her family. Sheila and Shane waited impatiently at the dining room door.

'Is that really why you don't want to go swimming?' she asked, more softly.

'Why can't I get undressed by myself?'

'You're too old for the ladies' changing room and too young to be in the gents' by yourself.'

'Why? I can walk around here alone.'

'That's different. Not all men are good. I've warned you about that.' Something about his open face made her feel sickened by the world. How long could his innocence last and was she right to destroy it by saying more? 'Is the attendant not nice?' she asked.

'He makes me go into a cubicle and pull the curtain so I'm alone inside.'

'What's wrong with that?'

'I feel odd alone behind the curtain.'

Alison drew him to her. 'We'll get you your swim some-how,' she said. 'Leave it to me.'

'I miss Daddy.' His voice was muffled by her sweater.

'I miss him too. Now how about that milk you're dying for and a nice big fry?'

Danny ran ahead, pushing the door open and ushering the others towards their table. He had ordered for them all before Alison even sat down.

There was no way you could enjoy breakfast with three children to mind. Spilt milk had to be wiped up and sausages cut. Sheila just ate toast and milk because of her throat and enjoyed being fussed over by the waitress who had heard about last night's scare. Danny was on his best behaviour, enjoying the role of family elder.

There was a reason, of course. He wanted to be out of doors as soon as possible. He pushed his half-eaten breakfast away before she'd even got the chance to touch hers, and offered to mind the others.

'They're not finished yet,' she said, to be greeted by a Greek chorus of Shane and Sheila crying, 'We are.'

'You have to rest your stomachs. You can't jump up,' she argued, but knew it was no good. They had been constrained in the bedroom already, it was impossible to keep them still. The sun was shining with no breeze, but she was concerned for Sheila. After last night she'd have happily cuddled the girl on her knee all day, but Sheila was a bundle of energy again. She warned Danny to keep her in sight, then let them loose, resigned to eating breakfast alone.

Joan waved, herding her brood from a nearby table. Alison smiled across, determined to start the day afresh. Mr BMW passed with his exploding hormones of daughters.

'Has he done a bunk or is he washing dishes in the kitchen?' He threw his head back to laugh at this startling witticism. Alison smiled, icily, thinking that chemical castration would be too painless for him, and, when he moved away, she noticed the small table in one corner where Chris Conway sat, watching her.

So he hadn't booked out or maybe he was finishing

breakfast first? The surge of pleasure she felt confused her. It would be simpler if he had departed, if last night could be left to stand alone in her mind. He rose, wiping his mouth with a serviette, and made for her table.

'How is the patient this morning?' he asked.

'She's fine, full of life. Thanks again for helping.'

He lowered his voice, leaning forward so his hands rested on the table. Anyone watching might think they were conspirators.

'I want to apologise . . . if I did or said anything to disturb you.'

'Chris, let's just forget . . .'

'I know. I'm just not used to letting anybody get close.'

He glanced around at the last few couples enjoying their breakfasts. She noticed the Irwins, Mrs Irwin especially, watching them.

'Back in Dublin it felt like I was drowning in concern. That's why I've travelled so much, hardly sleeping in the same place twice. It's not that I haven't enjoyed meeting you, but there's less pain in being anonymous.'

'Is that why you're leaving?'

'Do you want me to go?'

Whatever Chris did should not concern her. Alison had enough concerns. She wanted no repeat of last night, but these snatched moments talking to him felt like a tiny air pocket in which she became an individual again and not just someone's mother or wife.

'No,' she replied. 'Not on my account.'

'I didn't sleep much,' he said. 'I was up early, down on

142

the beach. The blueness of the blue waves, everything looks so special.'

'Why?'

'A different light. I might stick around a while longer. But you won't be upset if I decide to slip off?'

'No,' she said.

'It's just that I've told you things I've told no one else. But it's not fair on you. You've your own kids to mind.'

His concern annoyed her, for being unconsciously patronising. Part of him hadn't changed.

'My kids don't own me now, any more than Peadar did twenty years ago. Why must you always decide things in advance for me? Maybe you find it chivalrous but I think it demeans me.'

He scratched his chin. 'Well, that puts me in my place.'

'I simply want you to see me in my own right.'

'I see you getting hurt if you're not careful.'

'You hurt me once before.' The Irwins were leaving, Mr Irwin taking one last glance back.

'I never did anything,' he said.

'Exactly.'

He sat down, smiling ruefully. 'Was I that bad?'

Something in his voice made her laugh and brought back how easily it used to do so.

'You were worse.'

'I wasn't used to being around girls,' he said. 'I grew up in an apartheid society. Then suddenly I got a job, sharing a tiny space behind the counter with the most beautiful girls.'

Alison smiled. 'That must have been hard.'

He shook his head ruefully. 'I'd no sisters, no experience

of the opposite sex. The different smells, hair sprays and per-
fumes, and sunbathing out in the yard in summer. The way
girls talked, their different laughs, your laugh especially.'

'What was it like?' Alison felt charmed now.

'You'd try to act all grown up, telling dirty jokes, then
forget the punch-line or go into a fit of giggles, blushing
furiously in the middle of it.' He looked at her. '*There was a
young man from Sneem . . .*'

'What?'

'I remember you still, sitting up, swinging your feet in
the van, reciting it in a Waterford accent.'

She thought for a moment, then it came back.

> '*Who invented the wanking machine.*
> *On the thirty-ninth stroke*
> *The fecking thing broke*
> *And it whipped his balls into cream.*'

Her face went red as she smiled with him. A waitress
came to clear the table. Alison glanced down, hoping the girl
hadn't overheard. She moved away and Alison looked up.

'I didn't know it back then,' Chris said. 'I was too nervous, but I love the company of women.'

'Did you stay long?'

'Six years. You wouldn't do six years now for armed
robbery.'

'You must have had your pick.' She found herself teasing
him.

'There were nights,' he said, 'the sort you have when
you're young. The details get jumbled up, but a few stand

144

out. Once in Clondalkin library with two blankets and a bottle of gin among the non-fiction.'

'You did not?' Alison laughed.

'Not to mention a night locked in among the rare Y-stock in the mobile library book store. Remember those long shiny tables, cool on a summer's night?'

Alison shivered. 'That place gave me the creeps.'

'A Cork girl who liked adventure. Making Irish coffees down the cellars with crumbling boxes of books around us. Eileen Delaney found us.'

'That old witch?'

'Eileen was an intelligent misfit. She kicked a borrower once in some posh branch library. They couldn't sack her, so she was banished into the dungeons of the book store.'

Alison recalled being forced to visit the old woman's lair. Passing through the book store that smelt of wax and stale air, and stooping to enter the cellars where an old woman's clothes hung on makeshift lines to drip-dry. Eileen Delaney always frightened her, appearing in shabby cast-offs from behind a wall of cardboard boxes with several cats at her heels.

'What did Eileen say?'

'"I'd kill for a cuddle myself." Then she saw the whiskey and cackled. The three of us sitting there, drinking Irish coffees at dawn.'

'People never really talked to her,' Alison said.

'We were too young,' Chris replied. 'We didn't want to know. She died in that book store. Glue sniffers set it alight. They didn't know anybody was in it. Neither did the firemen till they found her body, cradling two dead cats. Youths in Ballybough were stoning her cottage. She'd started sleeping in the book store with a fortune lying idle in the bank.'

'Oh my God.' Only Chris had taken the time to know her. His face seemed younger and more alive than yesterday. She knew why Jane must have fallen in love with him.

'You became quite a Romeo,' she teased.

'I only ever fell in love twice.' He gazed at her as Danny led the charge back into the dining room, saving her from having to reply. Her children careered between the empty tables, with Shane demanding to go swimming.

'You've got your hands full.' Chris rose. 'I'll leave you to it.'

'Come for a swim too.'

'Not this morning. Besides, I can't swim.'

'A sauna never hurt anybody,' she bullied, nodding discreetly towards Danny. Chris looked around, understanding. Alison rose, ruffling Danny's tangled hair. 'This is an old friend of Daddy's,' she said. 'You may as well wander into the changing room with him.'

It was no lie. The odd thing, back then, was how Chris went out of his way to become friends with Peadar. It almost seemed another way for him to feel close to her. The libraries had Dublin's worst soccer team, perpetually in search of bangers. At the first party she brought Peadar to, he had got coerced into playing for them in the County Council Cup and told to give his name as John Maguire, an elderly mobile driver, if booked.

Alison had cycled out to see them play the sanitation

department in Fairview Park, with Chris in goal and Peadar immediately asserting himself as a midfield general. The muscular binmen of the sanitation department led by double figures before half time. Ten minutes from the end Peadar lunged at one in frustration and the referee opened his book.

'Don't tell me,' he'd said, 'you're John Maguire. The last two I booked were as well.'

Alison smiled at the memory as she emerged from the ladies' changing rooms to find Danny and Chris playing in the shallow end of the pool. There was a tenderness in the way he played with Danny which she found difficult to watch.

Sheila was warned that she could only stay in the pool for five minutes today. Alison had brought her dressing gown and knew the child would enjoy wearing it as she pottered around the poolside.

Chris climbed from the water as she waded down the steps. It was almost like he was being careful not to be seen with her. Danny immediately paired off with the twins, indulging in clandestine spying on the old swimming instructor and his equally old pupil – though not even Alison could fathom exactly what crime the gang had decided they were engaged in.

She fussed over Sheila, watching Chris chat to two men in the jacuzzi. With his chameleon quality, he seemed at ease discussing anything from the stock exchange to farming. Joan's walrus-bellied husband, Joey, emerged from the steam room and joined them. She wondered if Chris would sense his wife's disapproval, but suspected that Joey's smalltalk rarely rose above his despairing addiction to Dundalk Football Club.

She noticed the start of a bald patch as Chris bent to

listen to whatever Joey was saying. She could still remember him hanging intently onto Peadar's every word in Gaffney's pub across from Fairview Park after that match against the sanitation department. From the moment they trooped into the bar he had cosied up to Peadar, insisting on buying the first round even back then. She had already noticed this effect Peadar had on other men who enjoyed forming manly huddles around him, with less assured lads like Chris grateful to be allowed to converge around the fringe.

The absence of any apparent rivalry with Peadar had surprised her. She'd already sensed Chris's attachment to her at work and spotted his funereal look when Peadar kissed her after the game. In truth she'd only met Peadar two weeks previously in the Cat and Cage pub and her initial attachment had been mainly relief at finding a boyfriend as tall as herself. But they could have been celebrating their silver wedding from the way Chris behaved.

That Sunday in Gaffney's pub Chris had volunteered to play in goal for Peadar's team at the teacher training college. During the following weeks he never found the courage to cross Peadar by asking her out, but had compensated by spending two nights a week drinking with him, the first man to sleep with her. This used to disturb her as she lay in Peadar's small bedroom on campus and knew that Chris had sat on the bed the night before, thinking about her as he drank into the small hours.

Had he still thought about her during the months following her miscarriage, when word must have reached the libraries that Peader and she had broken up? There were mornings when she had finished a night shift at the hospital and cycled out to that same bench where he used to sit on Drumcondra Road, pretending to read her paper as she waited for the fleet of mobile library vans to pass. It hadn't happened often, just at her most insecure, when she wanted to give Chris a second chance to tell the driver to pull over if he passed. Not that she was making a play for him, but – with ward sisters abusing her and slow crucifixions being suffered on dance floors – it was hard not to wish to recapture the heady sensation of being at the centre of somebody's world. Yet no van had ever stopped for him to run back calling her name. Perhaps Chris had never spotted her there or maybe after the miscarriage she was tainted goods?

Certainly, during those three years alone, there had been nights of biting loneliness. But why had she married Peadar so quickly after he found her again? She didn't regret her marriage, it was just that, looking back, twenty-two seemed so young, when she was only finding her feet as a person.

Joey was leaving the jacuzzi, with foam dripping from him. Chris glanced towards her. She nodded to indicate that Danny would be ready to get out soon, knowing she would never ask Chris if he had seen her on Drumcondra Road all those years ago. She would never discover if Chris had chickened out a second time and he would never know how close he might have come if he'd only had the courage to try again.

———— ❧ ————

It seemed ridiculous not to ask Chris to join them for lunch. The boys were bored of the huge buffet already. They would have been happier with chips and a bread roll, but the all-in price of the holiday was so expensive that she found herself piling up their plates.

Sheila looked down the long buffet tables brimming with delicacies and declared that she only wanted Weetabix. It was Chris who coaxed her into trying new foods, turning it into a game that had the girl laughing. Last night it was clear that Sheila had taken to him. For himself Chris simply picked some salmon and salads, asking the waitress to charge a half bottle of red wine to his room.

They chose a table on the terrace, even though it was windy. But Alison knew the children would scatter once they'd had milk and a few mouthfuls of food. It was simpler out here than having them run in and out. Danny saw the twins playing crazy golf and picked up a bread roll, ready to join them. She scolded him into at least eating some baked ham and said that he was going nowhere unless he took Shane along.

She was so busy keeping the peace between her sons that she didn't notice Chris playing the feeding game with Sheila. Her plate was divided up into a farm, with Chris making the noises of hungry animals as Sheila took bites for them and laughed at his running commentary. Anyone passing would think them the perfect father and daughter. This made Alison uneasy. His own food was untouched but the half bottle of wine almost finished. She let the boys go, knowing Sheila would soon demand to be allowed to follow them.

When the girl wandered off, Chris sat back, taking another sip of wine and toying with his fish. He looked at Alison.

'I'm sorry,' he said. 'I sort of took over. I didn't mean to do you out of a job.'

'You've a way with children.'

150

He smiled. 'It's amazing what they'll do for you when they're not your own.'

'Still, it must be hard . . .'

She let the sentence hang. Chris finished his wine, abandoning the food altogether.

'She reminds me of Rachel years ago,' he said. 'I had photos, taken in these gardens. Not her features so much, but the same smile.'

'Chris . . .' She touched his arm across the table.

'Do you mind me saying that?' he asked. 'Say if you do.'

'I don't mind.' She withdrew her hand before anyone noticed, busying herself with a knife and fork.

'It kills me not knowing how she looked at the end.'

'What do you mean?' She let go the knife and fork, folding her hands onto her lap.

'They didn't want me to see the girls' bodies. Jane's brother had already identified them. I saw Jane but, whatever state I was in, the doctors said there'd be no point served by my seeing the girls. They were wrong, I don't care what their wounds were. I wanted to touch their hair and hands that I'd kissed a thousand times. But there were so many doctors fussing around, everybody trying to do good, neighbours arriving at the hospital, priests, their head teacher at two in the morning. All I wanted was time to myself, just to sit with the girls, but nobody would let me. Later on some undertaker tarted them up to make them presentable, but they weren't my daughters any more.'

'You're upsetting yourself,' Alison said, though it was she who felt upset.

'I'm sorry,' Chris replied. 'I came here to remember

them at their happiest. I have the autopsy reports, details of wounds, but I lack the mental pictures. That means I keep inventing them, grotesquely. Not their flesh but their eyes, the different ways they might have looked at the end.'

'Please,' she said. The sun went in but it wasn't the wind that made her cold. She suddenly wished he hadn't drunk the wine, that he had left at dawn without seeing her.

'I saw the car,' he said, 'but even then I couldn't be sure it was mine. They had it at the police station in Dunleer. I gave the posse the slip around three a.m. and took a taxi. There seemed no point going home, or at least I hadn't the courage to. The taxi driver got freaked. I mean we drive fifty miles and I'm just standing on the roadway, staring through a fence at twisted wreckage. He fetched the cops. I remember sitting in some room with an old guard saying nothing, keeping me company. He brought me outside but I could hardly believe it had been a car once. It was madness, the terrible hope of some mix-up. Then I saw a scarf belonging to Sara and just knelt down crying.'

Joan and her brood came up from the beach. She glanced over in downright disapproval. Chris didn't seem to notice.

'The old guard drove me back to Dublin, offering to dispose of the wreck. I muttered a black joke to myself about Sam Burns hardly wanting it back and he said, "Sure, it's too far gone for even Sam to buy." I thought I was cracking up when he knew the name. "We all know Sam," he said, "we'll check the undercarriage if it's one of his cars. He's been known to weld whole chassis back together again."

'He asked had I not known that Burns dealt in crashed cars. But in my heart I had. The sly fuck with his mobile phone and allegedly pregnant wife. That car was too spotless for the potholes of Leitrim. But I'd got greedy. Everybody loves a bargain.'

'You said the crash was the other driver's fault?' Alison reminded him.

'A crash happens so fast you never really know. One second can make the difference between sitting here alone or having my family around me. The guard kept talking about Burns. Picking up wrecks at auction, selling them six months later as good as new. Sometimes there were complaints, engines seizing up, but mostly the cars had no connection to their numberplates. He's one lock-up in the Republic, another in Belfast. It's simple, buy a wrecked car, then stick its plates on another one stolen in the other jurisdiction. Change a few chassis numbers and who can spot the difference?'

Shane climbed onto the waterfall and balanced like an explorer surveying a new kingdom. Alison wanted to call out, but felt unable to break the spell of this conversation.

'So your car was probably just stolen,' she said, as though that was some comfort.

'I don't know what I sent my family out in,' Chris replied. 'But I tracked him down.'

'Who?'

'Burns. To the scutteriest yard imaginable with a hideous bungalow beside it. Miles of state forestry blocking out the sunlight, with no undergrowth, not a single living thing. He'd two Alsatians chained in his yard and bits of car parts every-where. Tyres and batteries, rusted exhausts. I kept thinking of an abattoir, slabs of rotting meat. It was three weeks after the funeral, I couldn't get their bodies off my mind. He wasn't there of course, off buying or selling. A salesman after my own heart. His wife was bringing the kids home from school in the battered wreck he allowed her. They were fabulous kids. You could tell she was bringing them up well. It didn't seem fair, the bastard having kids and mine dead. But nothing seemed fair then, a rage inside me. I needed someone to blame.'

'What were you going to do?'

Shane climbed down, but Alison was uneasy. What did she really know about who Chris had become?

'I just wanted to confront him with the consequences,' he replied. 'I wanted him to suffer guilt. I wanted to ask, man to man, would it have made any difference if I'd bought a car from a reputable garage? Maybe I wanted somebody to lift this guilt off my shoulders.'

'And did he?'

'His wife bundled the kids indoors, then approached like I was a strange animal. I asked about her pregnancy, laying on the sarcasm. But she wasn't having it. "What do you want?" she said. "I've children inside. Why are you frightening them?" That's who I'd become. Take away a family and you're left with the solitary man our mothers warned us about. I said I want to know the history of the car my loved ones died in. Surely I had that right?'

He went silent. Inside, people were gathering around the dessert selection. You couldn't feel hunger listening to this, but Alison would have killed for a white coffee, loaded with sugar for comfort. Sheila returned, looking at her with such an adult expression that Alison couldn't help smiling. She climbed possessively onto her mother's knee.

'You're always talking,' she told Chris. 'All you do is talk.'

Alison winced at Sheila's unconscious echo of the words she had taunted him with in Loughshinny twenty years before. But Chris only laughed.

He leaned down conspiratorially. 'Do you know my real name?'

Sheila shook her head.

'Mr Dull.'

Chris's tone changed. He was a natural storyteller. Alison couldn't tell if he was inventing the story or had told it to his own daughters. But within seconds Sheila was mesmerised, laughing at Mr Dull's adventures as pilots on aeroplanes and bank tellers fell asleep when he spoke to them, so he had to land planes alone and help himself to cash. Alison left them and joined the dessert queue. She glanced back out, again unable to disguise an uneasy feeling. She knew what the car dealer's wife had felt. Men alone, unattached, near children. She filled a tray with coffees, cakes and milk for Sheila and walked back.

Sheila drank her milk greedily, ignoring the cakes. 'That's better,' she announced in a grown-up voice and ran off. Chris watched her go.

'She's a lovely kid.'

'I'm sorry if she brings back memories.'

'Children are themselves,' he replied. 'It's not fair to put ghosts on their shoulders. I'm learning to let go. That's what coming here was about. The world doesn't stop because of one accident. People have their own lives, in truth they haven't time for someone else's grief.' He sipped his coffee. 'I owe Sam Burns for teaching me that at least.'

'What did Burns say?'

'I liked his wife. I couldn't help it, a Galway woman. You know how you get a feel for people, that there's somebody else behind the poxy hairstyle and Joe Dolan records, somebody who found themselves trapped into being Mrs Car Dealer with the longest phantom pregnancy in history. The sort of woman who puts up with things for the kids. She hated his guts, but would never admit it, even to herself. She asked how long it was since I'd eaten, forced me to go in and made tea and sandwiches, talking all the while with the kids in the front room at their homework. It felt nice, sitting with a stranger. I didn't want trouble, I'd decided to finish my tea and go. I think she'd half forgotten Burns because she looked as surprised as me when he appeared. I hadn't time to say anything. Maybe it was the sight of us so cosy, or his wife's guilty look, but he went for me – not physically, just shouting. I'd no right to be there, it wasn't his fault if my wife couldn't handle the bloody car. It didn't matter if he was a dealer. His cars were clean.

'It wasn't anger in his eyes, it was hatred. And I felt it in the room. In his kids who came to the doorway. The younger two hated me without knowing who I was. But the older two, they hated him. I walked out, shoulder to shoulder, both waiting for the other to throw a punch. The hatred left his eyes. He'd seen the intruder from the door. I could drown myself in the nearest lake for all he cared. His eyes at least were honest. Honest indifference.'

Chris stood up. 'I'm going to lie down,' he announced. 'Wine in the afternoon? Is there no end to my descent into decadence?'

He moved quickly away, before she could speak. The

Bennetts were coming out, with putters in their hands. Chris held the door for them. Mrs Bennett smiled in appreciation. Alison felt cold. She looked in the sandpit for Sheila, then found her alone in the playroom, colouring in a picture. Some child had run riot in the pretend kitchen. The plastic cooker and fridge were overturned, with pots scattered on the floor. Alison picked Sheila up, despite her protests and carried her outside. She sat on a bench, rocking her, humming snatches of tunes, needing to feel the warmth of her daughter's body and be out among ordinary people in the sea air.

---

Alison needed to escape from the hotel. Maybe to the National Heritage Park at Ferrycarrig, where the children could run loose along the woodland paths between replica Neolithic farmsteads and ring forts, or simply to walk along the lake at Johnstown Castle.

Yet she was stranded, a prisoner without a car. Jack Fitzgerald would arrange a lift into Wexford if there was something necessary to purchase. But she couldn't simply say that she needed to get away.

At four o'clock, after giving Sheila her antibiotic, she rounded up the children for a walk on the beach. Danny was being belligerent, claiming he wanted to stay, but she couldn't risk leaving him on his own. Besides she wanted her family around her, doing proper family things. She had fantasised about them walking together like this and for once reality wasn't going to ruin the fantasy. They'd walk along the beach and be happy if it killed them.

And they were. Within minutes sulks were forgotten as the boys threw stones into the waves and carved their names on wet sand. The beach curved for miles, all the way into Wexford town with its twin steeples in the distance. Sheila collected coloured stones and shells for her bedroom. Alison's pockets were lined with sand as she minded them.

The further from the hotel they went, the more carefree Alison became. This was what a holiday was about, even if Peadar wasn't here to share it. The perfect greeny-blue of the sea, the miles of deserted strand. No doubt the weather was better in packaged resorts abroad, but there was nothing personal about them. Childhood was so short and memory so fickle that she wanted to give her children a few perfect images to carry through life.

But you couldn't choose what children would remember. Maybe in thirty years Danny would only remember the sensation of being sick in a hotel bathroom; Sheila might recall her mother's terror as she was dragged into hospital in the dark and Shane might still experience the sensation of feeling abandoned as his brother deliberately hid from him with new friends.

Would they still be close then or have scattered across the globe? The future frightened her, technology changing so fast it was impossible to imagine their adult world. As always on this beach, it was her parents she began to think of, their hopes and disappointments with her and how they would have loved to see Sheila run along the shingle with sunlight in her curls.

As always Danny was the first to want to turn back, sitting on a rock to ask if she remembered to bring drinks.

Shane was sturdier, with more stamina. Alison would have walked forever. The horror of Chris's story seemed distant now, as did his kiss last night. This was her life, in its here-and-now wonder. Danny took her hand, trying to steer her up the dunes where he guessed there were roads with shops where drinks could be cajoled from her.

'I wonder will Daddy get down soon?' he asked.

'You miss him, don't you?'

'It doesn't feel like a proper holiday.'

'We'll make it one, eh.' She gave him a squeeze. She could remember him being born and the strange relief that he wasn't a girl. A fresh start.

'He must be lonely without us,' Danny said.

'I'm sure he is.'

'At least he said my painting of the windmill was cheering him up.'

'What painting?'

'The one in the kitchen, beside the phone.'

'What did he say?' Suddenly goosebumps appeared on her legs.

'That he was looking at it as we talked and I told him I'd made the sun especially bright to cheer him up.'

'Walk on ahead,' she said. 'To the top of that sand dune. See if there's a shop along the road.'

Why in God's name had she walked so far? Why in God's name was she such a bloody fool? Imagining the perfect anything. If Peadar was at home this morning then he definitely wasn't there alone. She remembered clearly how his voice changed in the way it always did on the phone when someone entered the room. It couldn't have been McCann or a solicitor. Peadar never arranged business meetings at home. He said they made you look like an amateur. So who the hell was walking around her kitchen at eight-thirty a.m.? What little tramp, still naked maybe except for her dressing gown. Showering with her soap, her towels, making love to her man. It was irrational, these sudden accusations taking root in her head. There were no previous signs but no apparent signs in Ruth's marriage either. Not that Alison would have known what to look for. Ruth always said that the wife was the last to know, emphasising the phrase whenever they met for coffee. Alison had thought this was dramatic self-pity, but maybe Ruth had been trying to tell her something that the whole of Raheny already knew.

Sheila tugged at her arm with another shell. She almost flung it back at the child, then caught sight of her daughter's face.

'Run on up to Danny,' she said. 'Help him find a shop. Go on, you too, Shane!'

She watched them run innocently across the sand. She had no other proof, just the intonation of a voice that she knew inside out. Peadar, her rock. Could she be transferring her own guilt about last night onto him? Herself and Chris were different. That had just been one moment of relief over-spilling. She stood alone, watching her children crest the dune. Danny pointed, calling back. Everything was still perfect, if she could only control her imagination. She wanted to sit on a rock and get her breath. Maybe McCann had called over, that man would sleep in Peadar's ear if allowed to. There was no proof of anything, no proof at all.

She could hear Danny shouting, 'Hurry up, Mammy,

hurry up!' Peadar wouldn't risk ruining their happiness. The children ran impatiently towards her, sliding in the sand. Danny led the way, her firstborn, the spit of Peadar in many ways. She put her hands out and he jumped up, pressing his arms around her, laughing and scolding at the same time that she was such a slowcoach in everything.

――――――◆――――――

The obvious thing was phone Peadar, but he never seemed to be in. Perhaps he was on his way down to surprise them – he loved surprises. But she didn't know where to find him in Dublin. The answering machine wasn't even on at home any more, as though he was deliberately avoiding people, and the school phone simply rang on.

She slipped away from the children's disco to try again from their room – even phoning his solicitors, but it was six-thirty and the office was closed by then. Who else could she call? McCann would only get pleasure from being rung up, his sly voice yielding information grudgingly with his countryman's habit of answering every question by asking a question himself.

It was only then that she noticed two slips of paper on the bedside locker. Shane must have picked them up when entering the room before her. They were messages from reception, obviously pushed under the door, informing her that Peadar had phoned twice while she was on the beach. 'All's well' read the first message and 'Sleep well' went the second. They read like a cheapskate's telegrams or clues in a cryptic crossword. She rushed back to the disco before the children missed her.

When they were watching their video with curtains drawn in the television room, she went into the French Bar. How long was it since she'd sat in a bar on her own? But this was Fitzgerald's where you could relax without people getting the wrong idea. She needed a rum and coke. Last night's guilt was getting to her, her imagination running riot. She wished she hadn't left her book in the room or had something to read, even one of the bloody kitchen brochures still littering the house at home. Another failing that annoyed Peadar – indecisiveness. What would it have mattered if her new kitchen had been of Scandinavian pine or American white elm? Even if they could afford to buy the bloody thing, any man would grow tried of somebody incapable of making a decision. That was another reason she had chosen Fitzgerald's instead – the safe routine was simpler. But maybe Peadar needed more, something she had grown too staid or preoccupied to give him?

The French Bar was empty. She loved its sense of evening light, the old display cases of exotic geese shot on the Wexford slobs, echoes left over from Fitzgerald's past, when guests wore plus-fours, brought nannies and enjoyed shooting trips. They would have been displayed here when her father worked in the kitchens – the White-Fronted goose, *Anser albifrons*, shot on the North slob in January 1934, and the Pink-Footed *Anser brachyrhynchus*, shot on December 2$^{nd}$, 1931, on 'only its second occurrence in Ireland'. So much for Irish hospitality, she thought.

The barman moved around, clearing the already spotless ashtrays. Alison was his only customer. If she wasn't there he could probably sit down and read his paper. She bought a second rum as much to give him a tip as for any other reason.

The kids were immersed in the video when Alison went to check. Sally was there, talking to another mother as she rocked her child. The young woman noticed Alison's surprise at her presence and walked across to join her.

'You stayed on.' Alison was pleased for her.

'Just about.' Sally lowered her voice. 'He's a queer hawk.'

'Who?'

'That friend you're always talking to. Chris something or other. Did you say something to him?'

'About what?'

'Us.' Sally jigged the child slightly who started to stir. 'You mean he didn't tell you?'

'Tell me what?'

'Then maybe I shouldn't either. This is our first holiday since the baby, our last for a long time too I suspect. My husband got talking to him once in the bar, just for a moment. He checked that our room wasn't booked for the next two nights, then paid for us to stay on himself.'

'You're joking,' Alison said.

'He didn't even want us to know, except that we refused to stay unless Jack Fitzgerald told us who it was. He's separated, is he?'

'Something like that.'

The baby was awake now, fists going, clamouring to be allowed to crawl. Sally struggled with him and laughed. 'He's gorgeous, isn't he? You won't tell your friend I told you.'

It was typical of Chris, Alison thought as Sally walked away. No fuss. An almost embarrassed generosity. She watched her children share one armchair in a contented tangle of limbs. That second rum was a bad decision. She decided to have no wine with her meal and maybe just an Irish coffee afterwards. The babysitter was due at eight but she took her time bringing the children back to the room. Lunch had been a casual, less public affair, but, generous or not, she didn't want to be seated at dinner before Chris Conway arrived and feel obliged to ask him to join her.

She didn't even try phoning Peadar as she got herself ready. If he wanted to talk then at least *he* knew where she was. With every evening the babysitter got chattier but Alison wanted to get away and not have to talk about last night.

The dining room seemed quieter this evening. Chris had either finished eating or not yet come down. She wondered if he had carried on drinking all afternoon. She treated herself to hot oysters with cucumber and butter sauce, then breast of Chicken Hibernia. The iced water was nice and she asked for a second jug. But it seemed to reactivate the rum in her system instead of diluting it. Jack Fitzgerald came over to check she was all right.

'Sally told me what Chris Conway did,' Alison said. 'That was nice.'

'It was,' Jack Fitzgerald agreed. 'He did it this morning when paying for himself.'

'But I thought he was staying till Friday?'

'He said he wanted to pay up front in case he slips away early. He's a free man, I suppose, able to come and go as he pleases.'

Alison finished her meal and walked down to the Slaney Room where tonight's band was setting up. It was a quarter to ten. Women from various groups smiled as if in sympathy with her plight, inviting her to join them. Their looks made her feel good about herself. But she went upstairs where it was quieter. Chris must have eaten earlier and now sat in his usual place. Feeling decisive, she ordered an Irish coffee for herself and another liqueur for Chris from a lounge girl before walking over to sit uninvited beside him.

The drinks arrived and they sipped them in what at first seemed like companionable silence. But Chris wasn't just quiet tonight: she realised his mood was sombre. It drained her of the nervous euphoria the earlier rums had caused. She saw herself more plainly, not as someone coping heroically with three children on holidays but a woman pampered by her husband's money in a luxury hotel. For all that people talked about valuing stay-at-home mothers, this was her true status here. Almost every other woman present held down an outside job, shunting children between crèches and childminders. They mightn't say it aloud but some even regarded her giving up a career to mind children as a sort of betrayal.

Out among the distant lights of Wexford town battered wives in hostels would kill for the chance to mind their children here. Mothers whose partners had died or done a runner. Coping with life's random throw of the dice. Happiness lost in one turn of a steering wheel or glance of temptation in a crowded bar. Surely Peadar wasn't crazy enough to risk their happiness? Was she? How much reassurance did she need that she still existed as herself? *Sleep well.* Maybe Peadar was driving beyond Rathnew now, with the dark mountainy road falling before him.

The band started playing. Chris hailed a lounge girl,

asking for the same again. The drinks came and he let the girl keep the change, though it was an enormous tip. But Alison felt it wasn't done to impress her, any more than his generosity to Sally had been. He hardly seemed to notice the money.

'Did you sleep this afternoon?' she asked.

'I don't sleep much. I can't bear the dreams.' He stared down at the dancers below. 'Often I'm in a car out of control, spinning. I look across and see three heads staring at me from the dashboard, convinced I'm going to save them.'

Alison put her hand across the small table. She touched his fingers, felt his wedding ring. She wanted to comfort him or maybe stop him talking. He allowed her fingers to rest on his for a moment. Then he moved his hand away.

'Not all dreams are bad,' Chris said. 'Some are just ordinary moments, walking them to school or cooking dinner. I don't know how long dreams last, but at least I'm with them that long.' He sipped his whiskey. 'The mundane ones are worse actually. Insidious. Creating such an illusion of normality that when I wake I'm not sure which world is reality and which is nightmare. That can be hard, the momentary hope you hate yourself for.'

Alison felt a sudden resentment, like she had been suffocating for days inside the vacuum of his finely controlled grief.

'It hasn't exactly been all roses for me.'

He looked across. 'I'm sorry,' he replied, 'I've become self-absorbed. But Peadar's done well, hasn't he? You always seemed made for each other.'

'Did we now?'

Her tone caused Chris to make a self-deprecating gesture.

'Peadar always knew what he wanted. He still does by the look of him. An express train going straight from A to B.'

'How did you know I wanted to go there with him?'

'Are you saying you didn't?' he asked. 'Surely there have been stops in between where you could have got off.'

There seemed a deliberate undertone in the remark.

'This isn't one of them,' she replied sharply.

'I don't know what you mean,' he professed. But his eyes unnerved her. Chris had always been incapable of moving in a straight line. Everything was a mental game of chess, where you never knew what was coincidental or planned. Maybe he'd expected Sally to tell her and manoeuvre him into a better light. She remembered him cajoling people into switching rotas so he could get out on a library van with her, then vehemently denying having done so.

'Did you know I was going to be staying here?' she asked.

'What?' He sounded genuinely surprised.

'Peadar and I always stay here on this week. Any staff member could tell you. Did you plan all this?'

'All what?' Chris was angry now. 'Did I drive Peadar's builder bankrupt? Tamper with my wife's car? You're in the bloody phone book, Ali. If I wanted to talk to you that badly I could have simply called.'

'How do you know we're in the phone book?'

He glanced away, in sudden check. 'Old habits die hard. Every year when the new phone book comes in I check. It's not spying, it's . . .'

'What?'

'Habit. Memory.' He looked back. 'I wouldn't have come if I'd known you were here. It wouldn't be fair.'

'It's a free hotel,' Alison said, then laughed at the irony. 'Well, free if you can afford to pay.'

'There's nobody freer than me. There's nothing I couldn't do now, nowhere I couldn't go. I'm a rich bloody man. I didn't even want the money my partner gave me for the business. Just sitting in the bank. Money from selling the company, from Jane's insurance policy and God knows how much the house will fetch. The type of nest egg you slave for twenty years to build up by skimping and saving. Now there's nothing I can think to do with it and no one to pass it on to.'

'Where will you live now?'

'Why?'

'I want to know.'

'I told you, I'm going away, starting again.' He beckoned the lounge girl. 'Have another drink.'

'The babysitter is expecting me.'

'Let her wait.'

'I don't want her to wait.'

'I'm sorry.' He ordered for himself and the girl walked away.

'I don't mean to sound so sharp,' Alison apologised. 'Sometimes Danny wakes with night terrors. I like to be there, just in case.'

'I understand. I'll sit up for a while.'

There was something vaguely comical about his apologetic tone.

'You do that. Enjoy your few drinks.'

'You know I stopped twice on the way here,' he said, 'even turned the car at Arklow and drove several miles back towards Dublin before I found the courage to go on. I'm glad I did now. It's the right thing. But believe me, my presence here has nothing to do with you. Remember that. Lives overlap, events recur but differently. I'm as happy tonight as I've been for a long time. These last days I've had time to think things through, very calmly. Meeting you has been wonderful, God alone knows how often I hoped we would. But we're different people now, driven in different ways. I want you to understand that.'

She understood the words, but not what Chris was saying. Alison stood up. He stared at her, as if requiring a response. She nodded uneasily and he smiled.

'Tuck those kids in tight, you hear?'

'I will,' she replied. 'Don't drink too much. Thanks for helping with Danny today . . . and for last night.'

He looked at her again in a way she didn't understand but felt she should. She had meant to thank him for driving to the hospital, not for the kiss. Or had she? Chris seemed about to speak, then looked down, deliberately absorbed in watching the flame flicker up the rolled tobacco as he lit a cigar. She turned and descended the stairs, past the dancing couples, and every step made her uneasier, filled with a foreboding she could not articulate. She was missing something, a clue buried in his words.

Alison paid off the babysitter and sat in semi-darkness, watching her children sleep. She missed Peadar, not just his company but his reassurance. She wanted the feel of somebody beside her tonight. She wanted to phone him. Her earlier suspicions were crazy. He would be working late with spreadsheets littering the kitchen table. She told herself that her voice might wake Danny, but this wasn't the real reason she didn't phone.

A last drink would help her sleep but she didn't want to leave Sheila alone, even for the time it would take to visit the bar. Room service would be too embarrassing, making her sound like an alcoholic. She kept meaning to get undressed, but fussed around instead, arranging clothes, fixing blankets, pacing around the bathroom, slowly driving herself insane.

What the hell was she missing? *Lives overlap, events recur but differently.* Trust Chris Conway to talk in bloody riddles. She sat on the stool before the mirror and took off her earrings. Her eyes looked tired. She removed the scarf from her neck and undid the buttons on her blouse. She had to confess that she had got dressed up for Chris. Meeting him again was like being forced to sit in judgement on herself. The reality of now versus the image he had carried about for twenty years.

At least in this half light the dichotomy did not seem so great. The mirror made her face and neck appear young. Her figure hadn't changed so much, she told herself, or at least not in this light. Her bottom was bigger but her breasts looked the same. Not that Chris would know. The closest his hand had come was three or four inches from touching them during that lunchtime on the beach at Loughshinny twenty years ago.

She wondered if he sometimes ventured those final inches in his mind, speculating on what could have happened next. There was red stitching in her bra that day when her T-shirt rode up in their horseplay. Red thread circling the pink-white cloth that was almost transparent. More white than pink or at least paler than the flushing pink of her nipple, visible to them both through the bra, erect in the sea air.

Chris had been a coward. Shyness was a polite word for pure cowardice. To have gone so far and then stopped, remembering she was somebody else's possession. Why then, if it infuriated her, did she still remember the moment so vividly? Why was it that occasionally in the years since, when Peadar sleepily reached for her breast, it was Chris's hand she wanted to imagine slowly circling her nipple?

Chris Bloody Conway. She couldn't even say that he was one of the few men with whom she'd actually had a relationship, not like the two she'd slept with, during her time apart from Peadar. The forty-year-old radiologist who had been her only one-night stand – how ancient he had seemed. Alison still didn't know why she had slept with him – just three weeks after breaking up with Peadar – except that it made absolutely no sense and she had told herself she was finished with sensible behaviour. But really there were three people in his apartment that night, as she imagined Peadar there, forced to witness her actions and accept she had a mind of her own, even if only for doing crazy things.

Stephen was different, six months later on, not just an impulse of revenge on the rebound. Stephen with untidy locks of curly hair and oil streaks on his jeans from his motorbike. The feel of the wind in her dress, tucked right up between her knees so that her legs were on display as she rode as his pillion passenger. She hadn't cared if Peadar or anyone saw her then. French kissing in doorways off Grafton Street at closing time, never knowing where his hands would stray. Making love in the Pine Forest above Rathfarnham. That irresponsible excitement, no longer being treated as a girl, but a woman. She'd had to go on the Pill. Peadar might have been content with condoms, even after the initial accident, but Stephen was having none of it. He had taken it for granted that she would look after that side of things, just like he took it for granted that she would happily perform oral sex. 'Jaysus, haven't I washed it,' he'd argue, 'what more do you want? If that bleeding ex-boyfriend of yours said he didn't want it then he was a bleeding liar. There isn't a man born alive not dying to come on the tip of your tongue.'

And she had done it too, done what she'd refused to do for Peadar, and grown, if not to like it, then at least to enjoy the anticipation of what would come afterwards. Even today she still didn't know enough about men to judge if Stephen was exceptional in bed, but something about his carelessness excited her like she had never been stirred before or since. It was in his indifference as to whether his housemates downstairs heard her cry out when he ploughed into her on Sunday afternoons, and the way he rolled their bodies over so the wet stain was always on her side of the bed when he came.

Half the time she hadn't even liked him and sensed that, at heart, he didn't care. One Sunday afternoon she had stuck a note on the bedroom mirror and left him as he slept after sex. She would have kept going too, back home to be consoled by her flatmates, if a bus had ever turned up at that poxy estate he lived in, perched in the foothills of the Dublin Mountains. After an hour shivering in the cold she'd had second thoughts and went back to give him another chance. Stephen hadn't even seen her note in his hurry to watch a football match on television. His big sleepy grin when she walked in, and then his baffled expression when he saw that she was empty-handed and hadn't actually gone out to buy more beer.

Her thoughts were disturbed by solitary footsteps coming down the hotel corridor, slow and undoubtedly male. What in God's name was she doing sitting up, half naked, thinking about other men? Had she locked her door after the babysitter left? The footsteps drew nearer, an even, cautious tread. It could be anyone, couples didn't always return to their rooms together. But she knew it was Chris. Why was he walking so slowly? And why did she still remember the unfelt weight of his hand not touching her breast, when she could think of Stephen now and feel only indifference? The sweat-drenched girl moaning in Stephen's bed was someone else, a brief-lived stranger. But, just now, Alison felt that the incarnation of the girl who lay on Loughshinny beach was still alive inside her, alongside the child of twelve being kissed on the strand at Fitzgerald's. Even her nipples felt as if sea air was stiffening them again.

She had taken her blouse off. Surely in God's name she didn't want Chris to enter? 'Thank you for last night.' Could he have taken her up wrong? He had endured four months of loneliness. Who could blame him for seeking some human comfort? She would not allow anything to happen, but supposing it did, would it carry this same sense of betrayal for him? Was betrayal of a dead partner as hard as that of a living one? Why was she even thinking like this, just because of one kiss? She had never looked at another man nor wanted the touch of one before. But Chris wasn't just another man. He felt like a ghost, the igniter of a phantom pain so ingrained in her life that she had ceased to be aware of it. The loss of that girl who she herself had been. Where the hell was Peadar this night and just what was he doing? Could she be certain of him or certain of anything any more?

Chris's words taunted her. *Lives overlap, events recur but differently*. But second chances didn't come with three children asleep in a room. The footsteps stopped, just short of her door. Perhaps it was the man across the corridor, checking his kids. But there was no click of a key. She wanted to check if the door was locked, but that would look worse if Chris opened it, like she was coming half way to meet him.

She sat silently in the shaft of light from the bathroom and waited for his next move. How far was his hand from the door? She closed her eyes. This was exactly how it felt twenty years ago, lying on Loughshinny beach in early August with sand clinging to her back and watching Chris kneel above her.

Throughout that summer his hair had grown so lank that – half teasing – she had threatened to cut it next time they went out on a van. Leaving for work that morning, she had brought a pair of scissors in her bag. Peadar hadn't phoned for two nights, too busy cresting his latest Everest. If anything was going to happen, then this was the day. Even the driver sensed the electricity between them, how their hands found ways to brush against each other as they served borrowers all morning.

At lunchtime she had placed a chair on the sand. The driver laughed, wandering down the deserted strand with a pitching wedge and golf balls. Chris could have been a good-looking guy if he took the care. Alison had given him a haircut she knew he would never have chosen for himself. It brought out the softness in his face that he tried to hide behind a tough-man stance. She had trimmed his beard too, though she longed to shave it off and see what he actually looked like – around fifteen years of age, she suspected.

But she never felt so close to him as when cutting his hair. The smell of his skin, the way his nostrils seemed to try to breathe her very essence in. Once or twice she'd turned deliberately so her breasts were inches from his face. Their horseplay was never more intense than when he chased her down the sand afterwards, her cadging piggybacks on his shoulders, each trying to throw the other into the waves. Alison stole his jacket, taunting him flauntingly until his rugby tackle brought her down. She had turned onto her back, laughing, and tried to wriggle free as sand caught her T-shirt and pulled it up. Her skin, how white her flesh was back then. Her favourite bra she had chosen deliberately that morning. And Chris's face inches from hers, his hands trying to pin hers down.

Chris had released her hands suddenly and she'd lain there, breathing heavily. Her breasts, her ribs, rising and falling. Eighteen years of age. Chris was twenty. His back arched slightly, his right hand descending almost against his will. The expression in his eyes, flickering between her breasts and face. Five seconds, ten. Was time in a car crash this slow? His hand had hovered in temptation, fingers outstretched. What would she have done? Slapped his face and screamed for the driver? Or let him kiss her and touch her breast? Perhaps kissed him back greedily, in the glory of that moment when they were young and life stretched away to infinity. A different life might have opened, away from the complexity of Peadar, with no pregnancy, no miscarriage, no abrupt death of her youth. Old before her time, that's what the other nurses sometimes said about her. Maybe he wasn't half the man Peadar was, but she would not have lived her life perpetually trying to keep up, mentally apologising for her lack of ambition. The touch you never stop aching for is the one you've never known. God damn Chris Conway, anyway.

Alison wanted to pick her hairbrush up and throw it at the door. How dare he stand in that corridor, his hand inches from the handle? He wasn't some adolescent now and neither was she. She grabbed her blouse, doing up the buttons with trembling fingers as she reached the door and pulled it open. She was going to tell him what she thought of his indecision, ask how dare he torment her, order him to leave her alone. But the corridor was empty. Chris had walked quietly past long ago, leaving her waiting like a fool, a middle-aged woman imagining herself to be a teenager again.

This time she got into bed and tried to sleep. There were sleeping tablets in her shower bag, but she was afraid to take one in case she wouldn't hear if the children called her. She reached for Peadar's pillow and wrapped her legs guiltily around it, as if his scent still lingered there. She blamed the four drinks, but how could she have half hoped, even if only for a second, that Chris would be tempted to try her door? Fantasy and memory spilling dangerously over.

Peadar was the only man she'd ever loved. Her adventure with Stephen was already over in her mind before she found the letters to confirm her suspicion that he was separated with two children and a wife in a mobile home. Stephen had been important only for making her appreciate Peadar again – even though there was pain involved in getting back together. But she never regretted picking up the phone the evening Peadar called her flat out of the blue, and she had tried to calm her voice while her legs refused to stop trembling.

Peadar's very absence made her think of Chris again.

What must he be feeling, alone in his room? Two single beds beside the double one, empty shelves which should be spilling over with holiday clothes. How could he cope with those absences? Then she cursed him for intruding into her loneliness with his all-consuming grief.

Shane was twisting slightly. She knew he wouldn't wet the bed, but he was a pliable child, calm when woken. She carried him out to the bathroom, encouraging him softly to do his wee. He piddled away, eyes closed, face absolutely beautiful. He stood up, waiting to be lifted and cradled into her shoulder as she carried him back to bed. She cuddled into him for a moment as he reached for his Paddington Bear and smiled, half asleep, when he found it. Then he was gone, back into dreams that were never bad.

Alison was more awake than ever. She knew what she was straining her ears for. It was twenty past one when she heard the soft pad of feet on the gravel outside. They didn't pause. She could almost imagine the route Chris was taking. Slipping through the tennis courts, climbing the wooden steps, wandering across the grass criss-crossed by streamlets and the slopes of the crazy golf course. She lost him in her mind after that. What the hell was he doing out there? *Lives overlap, events recur but differently*. Chris had said it so deliberately, like a clue for her to grasp. But not just yet, to be revealed at a later time. Why did she sense it would be too late then?

She had to phone Peadar. He would calm her down, tell her to be rational, this was no concern of hers. In the half light from the bathroom, she knelt to examine the bedside phone. Just two clips attached the receiver to the wall. She lifted the carpet and saw a length of loose flex bundled up there. Nail pliers would undo the clips. She unfurled the flex until the receiver just about reached the bathroom. She was able to shut the door and hunch down by the sink to dial the number. Peadar wouldn't mind being woken. He'd know from her voice she was starting to panic on her own. In fact he'd enjoy being needed, the sense of taking control. But the phone just rang and rang. She dialled again in case she'd been mistaken. He had the answering machine off, so why the hell wouldn't he wake up and answer it? Was he okay? Was he even there?

She knew suddenly that he wasn't. Stephen's voice came back, though it was years since she'd thought about him before tonight. *'If that bleeding ex-boyfriend of yours said he didn't want it then he was a bleeding liar. There isn't a man born alive not dying to come on the tip of your tongue.'* What did Peadar really want from sex? There was always more happening inside people than you expected. You needed to spend years with someone before realising you knew nothing about what went on in their heads. Or inside your own for that matter, the memories surfacing, rekindled desires you never even knew you had.

But, on reflection, she knew that Peadar wasn't having a proper affair – he simply hadn't the time if nothing else. None of this had been planned. The builder had genuinely gone bankrupt, but once the chance arose Peadar hadn't been slow in abandoning them. What could be better for his conscience than to leave them all in a luxury hotel?

He must have brought a prostitute back to their house last night. It was pure and simple. The girl wasn't even gone by eight-thirty this morning. Every unanswered ring of the phone seemed to confirm her suspicions that he was at it again tonight, cruising the canal or Fitzwilliam Square or, worse still, those bleak lanes off Benburb Street. It wouldn't be in Peadar's nature to visit a nightclub and pretend to be single. His pride mattered too much for the lies of a one-night stand. And he'd never trust those massage parlours in cellars, where he wouldn't feel in control.

It would have to be a pick-up on the canal, a teenage heroin junkie, with a knife in her bag or a pimp following the car. What the hell did he need to go to a prostitute for, but maybe it was for nothing special? Was it just to be with someone different, someone younger? Maybe he would produce a torch from the glove compartment and show her the blueprints for his bloody extension? Maybe Alison was wrong and he was simply out for a walk or holding a crisis meeting in McCann's house? He could even be driving down through the dark to sleep in the car park and surprise them first thing in the morning. Alison didn't know and the ringing phone tormented her, making her invent things she had never considered before.

Had Peadar ever been unfaithful, maybe during those teacher conferences? Who could anticipate when temptation might suddenly occur, especially if you found yourself alone, out of your routine in a strange place, with time for gnawing doubts? The disappointments, which you always expected life to eventually make up for, except that you suddenly found time was slipping you by.

Alison carried the phone back to the bedside locker, carefully replacing the flex in case Sheila tripped over it. She should have returned to bed but found she couldn't. Instead she stood at the French doors, gazing out at the unlit gardens.

Was Chris out there, watching her like a voyeur? Twenty years ago, when he spent whole nights on that bench on

Drumcondra Road, staring across at her flat, she should have been frightened but had known that he simply wanted to feel close to her.

Where was he hiding now? She pressed one hand clumsily against the glass. Was this a penance, a vigil? She tried to ignore the impulse but it took hold. If Danny was going to wake he would have done so already. Once Shane was lifted he never stirred again and the antibiotic made Sheila sleep soundly. Still it was crazy to leave them alone, even for a moment. What sort of mother stepped out into an unlit hotel garden, leaving her door unlocked? She didn't even know what she wanted to say or do if she found him.

Chris had nothing left to lose, nothing to even stop him raping her. How could she explain to Jack Fitzgerald, and then Peadar and the police, why she had followed him out into the dark? *Lives overlap, events recur but differently.* She was no child now, she was a woman frightened for his sake. She pulled her dressing gown tight, found her sneakers and unlocked the door. She looked back: her children slept peaceably. The door closed with the faintest click. She panicked and tried it to make sure she could get back in. Then she carefully crossed the gravel to the entrance to the tennis courts.

She brushed against the net and knew that the wooden steps up onto the lawn were ahead of her. Surely it made sense to call his name, but she climbed them in silence. The blackness frightened her. You could break a leg falling over hidden rocks and water. She imagined herself lying here until dawn with her children crying for her. She pushed on, navigating from memory, searching for any sign of him.

An eerie night-light caused a reflection of the surrounding water to shimmer on the polished wooden roof of the pagoda. But it gave her something to steer by and the knowledge that Chris wasn't nearby. She looked back at the hotel rising behind her like an ocean liner. An elderly couple moved about their room on the second floor, the woman removing her earrings while the man closed the curtains over.

She should go back to check her children. If Chris had been watching her room she would have found him by now. A series of wooden octagonal shelters lined the boardwalk. She knew he had to be in one of them. But whatever he was doing had nothing to do with her. The man was simply coping with grief his own way, so why couldn't she leave him alone?

Yet his kiss hadn't tasted of grief. It was about life and hope, his need almost tangible inside it, like a man trying to cling to something. Alison walked on, down the boardwalk, with waves flashing below her, the lights of the ferry terminal glimmering in the south and Wexford town to her left. The flashes from four distant lighthouses lit the dark sea, each with its coded signals. She paused before every wooden shelter, knowing she should call his name in warning, half expecting a hand to grab her. But Chris Conway was in none of them.

She was bitterly cold, the wind making a mess of her hair. She felt cheated and empty and stupid. Chris hadn't made a fool of her. Throughout this holiday she had been making a fool of herself. He was back in bed now after getting some air, oblivious to her having followed him without even knowing what she wanted. Adultery just this once before it was too late? Revenge for Peadar's lack of attention, for the mundaneness of her life? Or was it for someone to stop the rush of time and make her feel special again for one last miraculous moment?

The children could be stirring. What was the safest route back? She couldn't bear to be discovered if the night porter noticed a movement outside. That ruled out the easy route across the patio.

It was only as she turned to go back that she spied the figure on the beach. His clothes were so dark that except for the splash of waves around his feet she would have missed Chris Conway. The tide was up to his ankles. The waves must be freezing, but then she remembered him allowing his body to drop in silence into the icy plunge pool.

He was going to drown himself on the beach at Fitzgerald's. This was why he had paid in advance. What better spot was there? Not in the pool where staff might get into trouble for not noticing a lone swimmer in difficulties. At sea his body wouldn't even be washed up here. It might get carried for miles along the coast, with nobody's holiday spoiled. Few people would notice his disappearance. Jack Fitzgerald would report him missing and eventually a body might be found and identified, the inquest verdict left open. He would simply be a man who couldn't swim and had got into difficulties in the water.

Chris Conway was going to die before her eyes if he kept on walking. She was about to scream when he turned around. Had he seen her? Did he know that it was her, for a change, watching over him? But it would be impossible for him to make out her shape. He started walking back, out of the water and across the strand, making for the steps up to the gardens. If she remained there he would discover her and know she'd been spying. What could she say? He was getting closer, passing the rock that guarded the steps. If he looked up now he would definitely spot her.

Alison turned and raced along the patio, knowing she could be seen by any nighthawks still up in the Slaney Room, but no longer caring. She just wanted to reach her room, to close the door and draw her curtains before his wet footsteps passed softly along the gravel again.

# THURSDAY

lison had to get some sleep. The children would start climbing into her bed at seven a.m., then clamber out to quarrel and play before besieging the mattress, urging her to take them down for breakfast. She had to sleep, even if only for a few hours. Twice during the night she considered taking the phone into the bathroom again to phone Peadar. Wherever he had been, surely he was home by now and alone this time. But how could she explain following Chris out into the darkness or that she didn't even know if he was still alive? He could have cut his wrists in the bath and left a note for the porter along with a large tip for the girls who would have to clean the room.

She should knock on his door and ask to talk to him. Three times she blacked out into sleep to see herself walk naked along the corridor to his room, with doors opening for guests to watch and Peadar appearing in the gloom. Each time she woke with her throat dry, trying to rein in her imagination.

All she had to go on was her instincts. Chris could have paid Jack Fitzgerald in advance for a completely innocent reason. He might simply enjoy walking on the sands at night. He could have been drunk, unaware of how close the waves were when they rushed in around his feet. But everything she knew about his past confirmed her suspicions. *Events recur but differently*. A clue that Chris couldn't even be sure she would eventually understand. An absolving her of responsibility this second time around. They had never discussed the events of that night after their row in Loughshinny. Chris hadn't wanted to die, it had been a cry for help, an act of self-pity even. She might never have known about the overdose if Peadar hadn't told her. That was typical of Chris back then, to run to Peadar as some sort of surrogate.

In the fortnight between that single instinctive kiss in Dalkey and the trip to Loughshinny, emotions between them had been building to a conclusion. Even the cleaners teased her behind his back. Peadar and her were in the midst of a deepening row, their first crisis. She had wanted him to herself, but he seemed to expect her to slot like an appendage into his established social life, to sip orange juice among the scrum of would-be teachers in the Cat and Cage and be happy to bask in his reflected glory as their natural leader. But being Student Union president in the college wasn't enough for him. His conversation was littered with plans for a position on the National Executive, for reforms and campaigns. There seemed nothing he wasn't going to shake up, a whirlwind in the making, a true son of the first president of the Teachers Union of Ireland to lead a national strike, someone whose ambition made her feel increasingly inadequate.

Twice that summer Peadar had asked her down to meet his parents in Oughterard. In July, for his mother's fiftieth birthday, Peadar had bought her a set of driving lessons in Galway. His father had laughed like it was a practical joke and tore the vouchers up before the whole family at dinner. 'Sure haven't I a car?' he'd announced proprietarily. 'If there's any-where she wants to go, then can't I drive her there?'

Not just this story but everything Peadar said about his

parents intimidated her. Alison never went down and Peadar was always different after he returned from seeing them, remote, tense, throwing himself into sport or study like a man desperate to prove something.

Not that there weren't times when Peadar made her feel special. Some nights after the hangers-on dissipated he had opened up with a surprising vulnerability other people never saw. At those moments she felt like the strong one and Peadar become a small boy, near tears, entangled between nets of guilt and expectation that she couldn't even begin to fathom. She had never met anybody more complex or contradictory, so that she felt unsure whether to be in awe of him or annoyed.

But increasingly, as that July led into August, she had often wished for a boyfriend whose attention she didn't have to compete for, somebody on her own level who made her the centre of his world. She wasn't sure if Chris might be that person, because he had never yet shown enough courage to win her respect. But in the days before Loughshinny she found herself tempting him, reading out the names of films that she knew Peadar wouldn't take her to and leaving pauses where Chris could ask her out to see them. Several times he seemed on the verge of doing so, yet the words were unable to come.

When she saw him switch the rotas so they would be out together on the Tuesday Loughshinny run, she had acquiesced to his plans, knowing that something had to give. But nothing did, except that – after the horseplay which felt like foreplay – she was left lying on the sand, momentarily half naked beneath him, exposed like a fool.

Poor Chris, forever crippled by shyness. But it wasn't pity she had felt that afternoon in the van, as borrowers came and went. She felt frustration and contempt. Chicken Licken Chris. She had turned on him, suddenly bitter. He was all talk and no action, better off at home playing with himself. He was only a city boy whereas she preferred proper countrymen. She couldn't remember half the insults she taunted him with, while he grew more morose and silent and the driver cursed them both, claiming he would never go anywhere with them as a team again.

Chris had got off the van at some traffic lights, not even looking back when she called, concerned now, anxious to make up. Previously whatever lay between them had been underplayed, so circumspect it was never visible enough to be broken. But something had frightened her about how he walked away between the moving cars like a beaten dog. The image still upset her that evening when Peadar had called and she deliberately picked an argument to send him away. She hadn't wanted any man's touch, she'd simply wanted to know that Chris was all right.

Next morning in work there was no sign of him and no sign of Peadar that night either. On Thursday Chris still hadn't appeared or phoned in sick. The sour-faced rodent of a librarian was thrilled. He always hated Chris and saw his chance to get rid of him unless a doctor's note arrived. Peadar had called to see her on Thursday night, apologising for not having phoned the previous evening.

'I was with your friend, Chris,' he said. 'Jesus, can that man drink. He turned up yesterday, looking like he hadn't slept. Six pints later he tells me how he crushed up ten sleeping tablets on Tuesday night and downed them with vodka. He's some headcase but I can't help liking him.'

'Why did he do that?' Alison had asked, feeling that everything was her fault and she would lose them both now.

'He didn't say, but he had that look. Woman trouble. Has he a secret girlfriend who's given him the bullet?'

'He doesn't have a girlfriend,' she replied.

'No. I rather thought he didn't.' Peadar had paused, studying her face. 'But that doesn't mean he's not in love with someone, does it?'

'How long have you known?'

'Sometimes when we're drinking alone he manages to get through a whole two minutes without mentioning you in some way.'

Alison had told him whatever she felt it was safe to say. She was nervous, unsure if Pcadar would feel angry or threatened. And maybe all along her intention had been to make Peadar jealous and force him to focus on her. But she was telling him nothing about Chris's feelings that he hadn't known already.

When she was finished he told how Chris had walked the streets all Tuesday night, waiting for the tablets to take effect, being almost thrown into the canal by cider drinkers, before, around four a.m., he had phoned a hospital casualty department. When he refused to go in they had told him to keep walking where people could see him, and drink as much milk as possible to flush the tablets out.

When he had told Peadar about the tablets on Wednesday afternoon, Peadar lured him onto black coffee and eventually coaxed him into visiting a hospital. He had stayed with Chris as the nurses examined him, even slipping anecdotes about Alison into the conversation so that Chris could talk about her, always in the context of a friend advising Peadar about how lucky he was.

The sleeping tablets had worked their way through his system by then. Peadar spent all Wednesday night with him, sitting up in a kebab shop drinking unspeakable wine. They had crashed in Peadar's room with Peadar insisting on Chris taking the bed. Alison had imagined Chris lying on the mattress where she and Peadar so often made love, still awake thirty-six hours after stepping off the library van, despite all the booze and pills. When Peadar woke on Thursday morning Chris was gone.

Ironically it was Peadar's concern for his rival which had finally convinced her that he was the man she wanted. For all of Peadar's contradictions she had known that she could trust him.

'He loves you a lot,' Peadar had said as they finished talking about Chris late on the Thursday night.

'Do *you*?'

Boys often use words glibly. But Peadar hadn't looked like a boy as he put his arms around her. He'd looked older than his years, strong enough to cure all her insecurities.

'I love you more than Chris does. If I couldn't have you then I'd try to kill myself too, only I'd do it properly.'

That was the night when the featherlite condom burst inside her. Peadar must have sensed it snap because he tried to withdraw, the semen splashing between her thighs and onto the sheet. It was four a.m. They were both exhausted, unsure of what to do next.

'I got out just in time,' Peadar whispered and, though she wasn't convinced, she had tried to blank the fear from her mind. Sleep overcame her and when she woke it was late and she had to rush into work. Chris was seated at the table and she ran over to hug him, knowing that he had inadvertently brought Peadar and her closer together, but unaware of Peadar's seed already moving inside her.

That was how Evelyn almost came to be born; how Peadar and herself split up but were drawn back together again; how her other children were later conceived; and how she came to lie awake in Fitzgerald's Hotel, worrying about a man who would never know the role he had played in shaping her life.

———— ⌖ ————

Alison didn't phone Peadar when she woke: she waited for him to call. When the phone rang the children were already in the corridor, hungry for breakfast. She let them play out there, not caring what noise they made. Every word Peadar said she found herself analysing, every intonation in his voice. The court had appointed a receiver, with a final site inventory to be signed off at eight p.m. Peadar would be a free man then, able to drive down late tonight or first thing on Friday morning for lunch and a swim before bringing them home.

She found the details drifting past as she homed in for any trace of falsehood in his voice. She wondered could Peadar detect the note of caution in her carefully phrased questions, her pauses each time she was on the verge of seeking advice. She had never thought she could be this unsure of Peadar or of herself. Where had he been last night and why was her hand trembling as she gripped the phone?

Twenty years before, Peadar had talked Chris Conway

away from suicide. She should tell him everything and insist he immediately come down. But – if her instincts were right – then what gave her the right to stop Chris? It wasn't an impulsive gesture this time. Chris was a grown man, rationally and methodically deciding his own future, bowing out as he wished. There were no dependants left behind, no loved ones to be hurt. This was no cry for attention. Few people would ever know so clean a death. What permission had she to ruin his plans?

Peadar was still talking away, annoyed by her lack of response.

'I'm giving you the choice,' he repeated. 'Will I come down late tonight or first thing in the morning?'

A door opened down the corridor and footsteps came.

'Mr Dull!' Sheila, who had been subdued since she woke, ran down the corridor. Chris was still alive. She watched him pass the doorway with Sheila at his side. He ruffled Danny's hair but didn't look in. Peadar's voice was angry.

'Jesus, woman, do you want me down there or not?'

'I don't know,' she said. 'Where do you want to be?'

'What sort of question is that?'

'An honest one,' she snapped. 'Remember honesty? What time did you go to bed last night?'

'Good Christ,' Peadar said, 'I went to bed when I was tired. I stayed in, sat up late, had a few drinks and a cigar. I didn't burn the house down. What the hell has that to do with anything?'

'You tell me. Tell me where we fit into all your bloody schemes. Tell me why I was phoning half the night and you weren't there. You tell me who you were with and what she does that I can't do!'

Alison knew she was being hysterical, mouthing half-formed suspicions aloud. Her anger was driven by guilt. Last night it was she who had imagined another's touch, who had wanted comfort, had realised how alone she felt, not just on this holiday but so often over the last year.

'Alison, what the hell are you saying?'

'I was never good enough for you, or your stuck-up father. I still see it in his eyes when we meet, the scrubber from the back lanes of Waterford whom you banged up.'

'For Jesus's sake!' Peadar was furious now. 'Are the kids listening? That was twenty years ago. Where the hell is all this coming from?'

'Drive down tomorrow. I wouldn't deprive you of a last night of freedom.'

'Listen to me —' Peadar sounded panic-stricken, but she didn't want explanations or excuses. Her outburst had shocked herself as much as him. She wanted time alone, to understand this crisis.

'The children are screaming for breakfast,' she said. 'Phone me later. I'd phone you if I ever bloody well knew where you were.'

She put the receiver down, shaking. Wherever he had been sitting up last night it wasn't at home. Danny came to the doorway, beckoning. She walked out, not caring if their hair wasn't brushed. For once in her life she was ordering strong coffee for breakfast and not tea. She'd order a Bloody Mary if they were serving them.

She would never mock Danny and his spy games again. All morning she was worse than him. Keeping one eye on Chris Conway, panicking if she saw him near the steps to the beach. One crazy golf hole overlooked both the deserted strand and the gardens. She kept playing it with Sheila and Shane until the children grew bored. The RTE executive and Mr BMW walked the course, analysing each hole. Danny came over to demand his morning swim. This time she let him get changed by himself.

Sheila's rash had vanished now she was using plain soap again. The antibiotic kept her throat at bay, but Alison couldn't get a word out of her. The child was cranky, near tears, just sitting in her robe on a poolside chair. Alison was uneasy until she saw Chris Conway appear. He made straight for the sauna, then after ten minutes came out and stood over the seven-foot plunge pool. Joan waded past, catching Alison watching him as he allowed his body to drop. Was this a dress rehearsal? Alison only let her breath out when his head and arm reappeared holding onto the ladder. He climbed from the plunge pool, shaking cold water from him like a dog, his stomach flat, shoulders strong, and walked into the steam room.

Alison had to talk to him. She asked Sally's husband to keep an eye on the boys, not even waiting to hear his reply, but aware of Joan's eyes burning into her back as her bare soles crossed the tiles to the steam room

It was empty apart from Chris. He lay with his eyes closed, oblivious to who had come in. The steam cycle was just starting, the room growing unbearably hot. Perhaps the thermostat was broken. Alison sat against the far wall and tried to recover her composure. She'd had a headache all morning, as always after a row with Peadar. God knows what he must be thinking in Dublin. But they were home truths she had spoken, even if he couldn't guess at the turmoil that was causing them. They had needed this holiday to put things right between them, to escape from that house and his job and all the other tediums and pressures.

Maybe lack of sleep was making her feel this fragile. She couldn't stay in here long with Sheila like that. Alison observed Chris through the steam. Perhaps she was wrong. He might have survived the worst of his grief and be starting on a journey back to life. Maybe he had been learning to let ghosts go on that beach last night.

'Chris . . . ?' He opened his eyes, surprised. 'Are you all right?'

'I'm fine, Ali, just fine.'

'If you ever wanted to call over, see us some time in Dublin . . . Peadar and I would like that.' Would they even be together in a few years' time? Peadar's parents had never broken up, they just refused to exchange a word in ten years, leading separate lives inside a single house. The morning that Peadar's mother had suddenly addressed her husband was viewed within the family as the first sign of her Alzheimer's.

'That's kind.' Chris's voice was non-committal.

'It was good what you did for Sally. Still you should be careful with your money, make sure you've enough for whatever you want to do next.'

She was trawling for some sign of any future plan. But it was like talking to a stranger. There was a new calmness about him, a serenity even. Whatever decision he had reached was one he was perfectly reconciled with. Alison was the tortured one, biting her tongue. Was it only three days since they had encountered each other here, two nights since they kissed and he told her she was the only person he still cared for? It felt like he was cutting her off now, carefully and deliberately. He had said all there was to say. This was surplus time, with every loose end tied up. All he had left to do was to kill himself.

'I'd miss you,' she said; 'if you were never in touch again.'

His voice sounded amused, gentle. 'Don't be silly, Ali. You haven't missed me in twenty years.'

The door opened. Two women came nosily in, complaining about the heat. She rose as they sat down.

'I'll see you later,' she said.

'No doubt I'll be knocking around. The proverbial bad penny.'

Chris made no sign of rising, yet his skin was running with sweat. It dripped from his glistening arms and legs, matting the hairs on his chest that she suddenly longed to touch. His face looked so hot she thought it would melt. She didn't know how much longer anyone could stand such heat.

All afternoon she wished to phone Peadar back, but pride and confusion stopped her. She wanted to try talking to Chris again, but felt unable to approach. He was ensconced at a table on the patio. Final entries for the golf scramble had to be in by three p.m. The Slaney Room was crowded with competitors returned from last-minute efforts to improve their scores, licking their wounds together.

There was a different feel about Thursdays in Fitzgerald's,

a heightened gaiety marking the beginning of the end. She even saw it in the children, trying to drink in every last sensation of the holiday. Danny would refuse to contemplate tomorrow's heartbreak until the time came to pack. Shane would cope with leaving as with everything, glad to be here, yet happy to see his own bed when they reached home. Sheila sat quiet in herself on the grass beside Alison's chair, idly fingering their room key. Whenever Alison urged her to go and play, the child barely looked up.

The women's crazy golf competition was finishing, with one or two serious-faced older women lining up putts as if fortunes were at stake. But generally there was an air of hilarity, with most women just out to have fun. The first male competitors were queuing to start their rounds, joking as well but with a different air about them. Competition was competition, male egos at stake. Jack Fitzgerald came out to watch, impeccably dressed as ever. Alison commented upon the difference and he smiled.

'Men will be men,' he said.

'I wouldn't mind but they'll let Heinrich win.'

'That's not compulsory,' Jack Fitzgerald said. 'It normally just works that way. I mean it's such a mad game nobody could seriously mind losing.'

Geraldine beckoned for Chris Conway to begin his round. Alison was aware of Jack Fitzgerald watching him too. Surely this was the time to warn someone, but what could she say?

'Do you think you'll see Chris here again?' she asked.

'I hope so. You never can tell.'

Jack Fitzgerald moved on as Alison watched Chris putt

expertly through the tunnel, leaving his ball inches from the hole. He walked towards it, plainly savouring the sea breeze against his face. Alison had never seen him look so much at ease with the world.

Jack Fitzgerald walked back towards her. If she interfered now then Chris would just go to some tacky hotel in a foreign town. Somewhere without resonance or memory. Death would be sordid there, a stranger cursed for his inconvenience. She would be tempted to kill herself too if her family died, but would fail to do so cleanly like Chris planned. Her death would be messy and embarrassing for everyone.

She looked down to find that Sheila had disappeared. The girl might have wandered off to play but the room key was also missing which frightened her.

Alison looked around for her. Shane was in the sandpit, involved in some complex make-believe game. Danny was off with those blasted twins, God knows where. Fear seized her. Nowhere was safe for kids, not even Fitzgerald's Hotel. Some stranger could slip up from the beach. A mother had to watch her kids. You had no right to become obsessed by your own cares.

She ran across to try the French doors into their room. It was locked with the lace curtains pulled tight. She couldn't remember if that was how she had left them. It was impossible to see in. She called Sheila's name, banging on the glass and starting to panic. Why would the child take the key without telling her?

Danny's voice startled her from the tennis courts. The twins were with him, clutching bottles of Seven-Up. He wanted money for one too.

'Where's Sheila? Have you seen Sheila?' she shouted.

The way he shrugged his shoulders infuriated her, a nonchalance affected to impress the twins.

'I asked you a bloody question,' she snapped. 'You have a bloody tongue on you.'

He stepped back, less sure of himself. 'Maybe she's on the beach.'

'Did you see her there?' The tide was coming in. Anybody could come along and snatch her.

'No. I just said maybe.'

'Don't just say maybe. Look for her.'

'Where?'

'Anywhere. Everywhere. You three are supposed to be the bloody detectives!'

She didn't care what the twins thought. She banged on the French doors again. Chris spotted her and abandoned his putter to run over.

'What's the matter?'

'Sheila's missing.'

'Try your room. I'll check around reception.'

Then he was gone, leaving his opponent stranded. She ran in after him. The corridor beside the dining room was empty. An elderly couple stepped from the lift, the woman on a stick. She brushed past, not caring how rude she looked.

If Sheila was in their room then surely she'd have come to the window? Her step faltered. Their door was half ajar. She pushed it open. The room seemed empty. Nothing was touched, not even her money on the locker. Sheila's ragdoll lay on the double bed and, on the floor beside it, Sheila sat with her knees cradling her head. There was no sound but

Alison knew she'd been crying. She approached carefully and knelt.

'Are you all right, pet?'

Sheila put her arms around her, her face blotched. How long had she been sitting there crying?

'Tell Mammy, whatever it is.'

'I don't want to go home tomorrow.'

'Did anyone bring you up here?'

'I wanted to talk to Daddy. You were busy. Why do we have to go home?'

'Did you come up here all alone?'

'You taught me our phone number. I kept trying to dial it, then some voice told me to put extra numbers in front.'

'But did you not hear me knocking on the glass?'

'I heard you shouting at Daddy this morning. You never let me tell him about the hospital. Why do we have to go home?'

'Because somebody else needs our room tomorrow, pet.' Alison lifted her daughter up. 'There'll be other holidays, lots of them. Year after year till you're a big girl and want to go away by yourself.'

'I'll never want to go away. I miss Daddy.'

'I know, but there's no point in phoning. He wouldn't be at home now.'

'No.' Sheila reached for her ragdoll. 'There was only men arguing.'

'What men?'

'I don't know. One said "hello", then another shouted not to touch the phone. He sounded cross. I got frightened and put the phone down.'

The child started crying again. It was a mistake, Alison

thought, a wrong number. Surely nobody had broken into the house. But could she be sure? She pressed the redial button to check what number Sheila had dialled. A phone rang, then Peadar's voice came on the answering machine.

'Go into the bathroom,' Alison told Sheila, trying to keep calm. 'Wash the tears from your face, close the door.'

The blips came, seven messages waiting, then silence.

'Whoever the hell you are,' Alison spoke loudly into the receiver, 'you'd better leave quick because I'm calling the police.'

She had almost put the phone down when a man's panic-stricken voice came on.

'Who the hell is that?' he asked.

'Who the hell are you?'

'Seamus.'

'Who the hell is Seamus? Have you got my husband there?'

'Is that Mrs Gill? You're not supposed to know we're here.'

'Am I not?' She was both relieved and furious. Whoever Seamus was, he sounded too rattled to be a robber. 'And who the hell says so?'

'Your husband. He told us to leave the phone alone. It's ringing the whole time. I think the fitted kitchen we're putting in is meant to be a surprise for you.'

She remembered Peadar's voice yesterday, changing as these workmen must have entered the room. God knows where he had found the money, but that was typical of his contradictions. It was also like him to do this quietly for her, just like he always had a coming-home treat for the kids. Still she wasn't a child to be fobbed off, if he couldn't explain where he was last night. Seamus sounded as concerned as if he'd given state secrets away.

'My apprentice picked up the phone by mistake to some child. I hope he didn't frighten her.'

'No, that's okay.'

She replaced the receiver. Chris entered the room. Sheila left the bathroom and ran to her.

'Is everything okay?' he asked.

'Everything is fine.' Alison hugged her daughter.

'Look after that princess.' He turned to go.

'Chris? Tonight . . . the last night . . . maybe you'd like to join me for dinner. I mean, it's crazy us both sitting alone.'

He looked back. 'Call me romantic,' he said, 'but I asked them to set the table for two. Absent friends. I hope you don't mind but I sort of like it that way.'

'It's a nice thought.'

'I'll pick a wine Jane would have liked. Still if you feel embarrassed on your own . . .'

'No, it was just a thought.'

Chris smiled and left, closing the door over.

'Do we really have to go home?' Sheila asked. 'Why can't things last forever?'

Alison sat on the bed and held her daughter.

———— ✍ ————

The magic show was on before the children's dinner. Alison brought Sheila down, making a great fuss of her and the boys. They could have as many drinks as they liked. She didn't care if they ate their dinners or not. Let them enjoy every minute of their last day. Alison didn't know if she would ever return. Not if each corridor reminded her of how she had let some-body, who once loved her, die here. When the show began she wanted to run back to the room. To phone the school, the solicitors, McCann, anyone who could track Peadar down. He would know what to do. Sally came across, shaking her head and smiling.

'You missed it,' she said. 'God, it was priceless.'

'What?'

'The crazy golf final. I nearly wet myself. That gob-daw with two teenage daughters was playing Heinrich. But he starts beating the poor lad, taking five minutes over every putt. He's four holes up after four. Another hole and he's won it. None of us can say anything with Heinrich present, not even Geraldine who's trying to drop hints. But the guy is oblivious. Then your friend, Chris, stands in front of him. "You're dis-turbing my concentration," the man says. "I hate this slope." "It looks flat to me," Chris says quietly. "As flat as the fucking tyres of your BMW."'

'Who won?'

'Heinrich, strangely enough.' Sally laughed. 'Your friend, he's so carefree. He doesn't care what anyone thinks, does he?'

The magician was calling for an assistant, scanning the forest of hands. Shane's was only slightly raised, half frightened of being chosen. But the magician seemed to home in on it, calling him up to cheers. Shane was given a hat that almost covered his eyes and told to hold a wand. Alison's name was being called on the PA system, a call holding for her. She got them to transfer it to her room.

She was out of breath by the time she sat on the bed to lift the receiver, half embarrassed by her earlier anger with Peadar, yet still unsure of where he was last night. Peadar couldn't mask his disappointment that she had found out about the kitchen.

'I picked the one you liked in the brochure,' he said. 'I wanted it as a surprise. I know things haven't been great between us lately, but I didn't know how bad they were until this morning.'

'I just wanted to know where were you last night.'

'Nowhere and everywhere,' Peadar replied. 'Places so silly I felt embarrassed mentioning them. I think it was seeing Chris Conway again that set me off, memories I'd forgotten about. From the first day we met I've envied you, you know that?'

'What do you mean?' she asked.

'Your ability to be content. I've never known it. All my life I've felt guilty if I'm just standing still.'

'You were always ambitious.'

'It's not ambition, it's running scared. These last months I've ignored everything except the blasted school. And I've seen it in you. You've been so quiet. Even if I touch your breast at night I can feel you tense up. I've made you unhappy.'

'It hasn't just been that,' she told him.

'I've been stuck between two worlds, only half paying attention at meetings because I want to be with you and then – when I am with you – driving us both daft with this guilt because I'm not at the school. It's always been the same. I can't stop pushing myself to achieve things I don't even want any more. I just want us to be happy.'

'We can be,' she told herself as much as him.

'This builder going bust at least gave me some time alone. Nothing to do at night but walk around sensing your absence, opening your wardrobe, fingering your clothes. I spent all last night out in Drumcondra. Remember your flat there and the streets and the park behind St Pat's.'

'You weren't in that park at night?' she asked, worried.

'I stood on the pedestrian bridge. That weeping willow is still by the river. The last time we stood there you were pregnant with Danny and you got scared that a child would change us, that we wouldn't still be here the same for each other.' Peadar paused. 'You sounded so cross this morning, I've barely been able to eat all day. Where did you think I was?'

'You know my imagination. I don't know . . .'

He was silent for a moment. She could hear the thud of tennis balls outside, distant voices.

'I've never . . . in all these years. I'll be honest, more than once I've been tempted. Other men telling me what they got away with, weekends in hotels. But I could never do it on you, even if we were separated. Last night I kept thinking of that summer we met. How young we were. Just you and me back then. That's all there will be again when the kids have flown. We need to keep it alive, you understand?'

'Yes.'

'I'd drive down to you now only I've had a few drinks. Here, in your new kitchen, which looks bloody marvellous if I say so myself. Will you be all right for another night on your own?'

'Peadar?' She didn't know how to phrase the question.

Once she mentioned her suspicions they would both be implicated, negligent in some way if Chris died.

'What, pet?'

'Supposing someone was going to do something and you felt you should stop them.'

'Something illegal?' he asked.

'Something you felt you should stop them doing for their own good.'

Peadar laughed. 'They won't thank you. People's good is generally their own concern.'

'But say it was something that would really harm them?' Alison was desperate to have this decision taken from her hands.

'I see it every day with parents,' Peadar said. 'People only ever learn from their own mistakes. I know who this is about.'

'Who?'

'Joan. If she wants to make a fool of herself over some man, then let her get on with it.'

'I didn't know whether to interfere or not,' she lied, suddenly relieved at a way out of this conversation. It didn't concern Peadar. This was her decision alone.

In the midst of her relief at his account of last night, she was surprised to find the tiniest, unaccountable spark of disappointment. Why did Peadar presume that she was always content with her life? Maybe her ambitions were more secretive, intuitive goals that he might never be aware of. When she was a girl sometimes in dreams she had found herself flying, soaring from the bed, not sure if she was asleep or awake as her hand touched the ceiling to steady herself. Her body tingling like during that first kiss all those years ago. The giddy sensation of specialness. That was what had become lost from her life. What did Peadar know of her or what did she really know about herself? Alison became aware of him again at the other end of the phone.

'There's something I should have told you,' she said. 'A health scare, but everything is all right now.'

She could hear the fear inside his silence.

'I had to bring Sheila to hospital, but it was just tonsillitis. Nothing to worry about. You get some sleep. I'm glad we talked.'

She hung up and sat for a long time, knowing that she would never tell him about the mammogram now. The magic show would be over soon, with medals to be given out. Peadar had not been unfaithful, he still loved her. So why did she still feel so desperately alone?

———— ◈ ————

Alison dined by herself. Perhaps Chris Conway had eaten earlier or not at all. Never swim on a full stomach. The macabre humour disturbed her. She ordered duckling à l'orange but it tasted of nothing. Couples were happy around her, unperturbed by what might occur on the beach later on.

There was an air of excitement around the Slaney Room. She went up the stairs to what she now considered as their table but Chris never appeared. People were up dancing to the band, anxious to make the most of their time. She walked out onto the balcony. The gardens were lit by soft light, waves crashing in a white line in the distance. Palm trees swayed. Below her the steps to the beach were empty. Perhaps Chris had already gone down there as soon as darkness came, unable to face one final meal, one last night of memories. He could be dead already, drifting out in the current past Carnsore Point or up towards Curracloe.

There was applause behind her. The activities manager had arrived to present the smaller prizes and then the holiday voucher for the winner of the golf competition. Alison walked back inside, hoping to spot Chris among the tables of drinkers. People were being called up to receive mugs for table tennis, badminton, indoor bowls, snooker, outdoor tennis and the table quiz. Mr Bennett had already collected three, with his wife one ahead of him. Heinrich was presented with a putter to a huge ovation, which dried to a trickle as Mr BMW collected his runner's-up plate. Chris should have been there to enjoy the moment. The band gave a drum roll as the golfing result was announced. With a good score on his individual round and a superb result in his scramble, including an eagle, the prize went to Mr Irwin. The man looked shattered as he walked up, his wife almost in tears. Quiet, decent people. Alison was glad Peadar had never corrected the mistake on their scorecard. This was what Fitzgerald's should be like, growing old together, resignedly and bravely, savouring tiny personal triumphs.

Mrs Irwin looked around to beckon Alison down. She knew she had to join them. They waited at the end of the stairs, holding the voucher like some sort of precious vindication.

'Let me buy you a drink, please, let me buy you a drink,' Mr Irwin was saying. 'That eagle made my holiday. The first in my life, but I went to pieces after it. It was your husband's scoring that carried me around.'

She had to stay for a drink and insist on buying them

one back. All their talk was of Peadar and how marvellous her children were. But Alison could hardly focus on their words, her eyes darting around the room. Nobody here even noticed Chris's absence. They had their own lives to lead. Ten forty-five. She excused herself but half the room wanted to talk to her. They'd noticed how well she coped with the children, they wanted her to join their groups, on her last night she shouldn't be alone.

She managed to escape into the empty corridor and almost ran past the dining room up to her room. The babysitter was watching television with the sound turned off, the children asleep. The woman was chatty, repeating every remark Shane and Sheila had made. Danny had been quiet, absorbed in his book. He was near tears, the woman thought, at the prospect of going home, with his giraffe now hugged close to his chest.

Finally she was rid of the woman and alone. Alone and trapped, although it was she who had rushed back to her children. To endure this night and discover tomorrow if her suspicions were correct. But how could she possibly sleep? She undressed and had the sleeping tablet in her palm before she stopped. Chris had looked beautiful in the steam room today. His arms and shoulders, the matted hair on his thighs, saturated with rivulets of perspiration. Twenty years ago Chris had crushed up ten of these tablets for love of her. Could she simply let him die?

She could knock on his door at least to check if he was there, claim she wanted to say goodbye in case he left early in the morning. Maybe she could talk him out of it, show him there was something still to live for. She sensed that deep down he must know that, from the way his eyes had undressed her outside the hospital. But what was she suggesting and how far was she willing to go? What would Chris think if she arrived at his room like they had unfinished business between them?

Alison had raised the tablet to her lips a second time when she stopped again. She could phone Peadar and tell him the truth this time. But whatever feelings still existed between Chris and her were private. Peadar was a good man, never unfaithful to her. But she wasn't Peadar, she was herself with her own needs, her own desires, her own decisions to make. Alison hurriedly threw on a sweatshirt and slacks, then checked the children. She would leave her own door open. That way Chris would know she could not stay.

The knock on his door was startlingly loud. She expected inquisitive heads to appear along the corridor. The second knock was louder but there was still no reply. She returned to her room and locked the door. Chris might be drinking in the Slaney Room now, oblivious to her, but still she couldn't settle. Something told her he was dead already. When she closed her eyes she could picture his naked chest floating on the waves. Alison opened the French doors for some air. She stood at the curtain and looked back at Shane who stirred slightly then settled again.

It was madness to leave them alone, to step from that room which contained her life. The gardens looked even darker than last night. A wind was up, tossing trees about. She fixed the curtains behind her, then closed the door, almost running on the gravel, blundering across the tennis courts. She grazed her knee on the steps, then stopped, unsure of which way to go. Lanterns among the bushes wove coloured patterns of shaky light, against a backdrop of vast shadows from waving branches. Her foot slipped into the water beside one of the golf holes. She fell with a muffled thud, trying not to shout. Complete darkness enveloped her. She had to navigate from memory, inching her way towards the wall by the stream to find the steps up onto the next tier. The boardwalk lay before her, with rope fencing protecting the sheer drop down onto the beach.

The crescent moon moved between wisps of cloud. The beach seemed deserted, with no trace of clothes, although the light was so poor that, at this distance, she couldn't properly tell. Grains of blown sand hurt her eyes. She had to look away, then try to peer back down. The moonlight was clearer for an instant. A solitary set of footsteps led to the water's edge. They become muddied in a churned circle of prints but no footsteps returned. She had almost turned away before a shape in the water caught her eye. But it wasn't wading out into the waves, it was struggling inland. Chris Conway staggered and fell, being almost swept back out by the waves before he found his feet and stumbled up the sand.

He collapsed onto his knees with his head bent. At first Alison thought he was giving thanks, then, even at this distance, she realised he was cursing his own cowardice. His clothes and hair were drenched. He struggled to his feet and faced the waves again. Was it really this hard to die, even when you wanted to, when you had nothing left to live for? This wasn't the first time he had tried to enter those waves. She knew that from how he stood, screaming in fury at them.

He looked back and she feared that he had seen her. But he was scrambling around, searching for stones. She watched him cram his jacket pockets with them. The tide was plunging in, already washing half his footprints away. He raised his head, then ran full pelt into the sea. When the waves reached his waist she saw him stop. She could almost sense his terror and self-disgust. What had she done with the lock of his hair? Every second of that day at Loughshinny flooded back to her, playing on the sand, both of them finding ways to touch as they pretended to throw one another into the waves. Everything building to a climax he could not deliver. Now here he was again, this time alone but still too scared to carry through his desire.

A huge wave caught him and he went down. She thought the stones in his pocket would prevent him from rising, but somehow his head re-emerged. Yet this time he didn't flounder back towards the shore. He walked out, calmly and slowly like he'd finally conquered his nerve. The waves were half way up his shoulders and then his neck. She found herself calling but the wind meant he would never hear. Then she was running, cursing the bolt on the gate, careering down the steps three at a time. The sand slowed her feet like running in a nightmare. She had three children asleep and a husband who loved her. It was crazy to take this risk but she couldn't turn back.

There was no sign of him in the water, only footsteps as a clue to where he had entered. She screamed his name, sobbing for him or for herself. She could have stopped him, she could have done something. After two decades of mocking his cowardice, she was no better. If she had really wanted Chris that day in Loughshinny she could have simply guided his hand to her breast, but she had been as much a coward as him. That was what had both attracted and repelled her, they were too much of a kind whereas she had needed somebody different to change her. Opposites attract. Whoever Jane had been, she would have resembled Peadar, practical and driven. Suddenly it felt that she wasn't just searching for Chris in those waves, she was looking for herself.

The waves were up to her ankles now when she glanced back at the hotel lights beyond the cliff. Nobody to see or know what might happen to both of them. She stumbled into the water calling Chris's name.

The water was bitterly cold, almost paralysing her. The force of the waves took away her breath. She stumbled and felt a shoe float loose. She was going to die if she did not turn back. This was sheer madness. A wave lifted her up and Alison found she was swimming, gasping at the cold, struggling for breath. All she had on was slacks and a sweatshirt. The sea water was sickening, stinging her eyes, pounding in her ears. She went down and thought she would never come back up. This became no longer about Chris, it was about saving herself.

She surfaced again, salt water filling her mouth as she tried to scream. The waves had turned her around so she was facing the beach. Her sweatshirt hampered her arms as she attempted to strike for shore. Then she saw him in the moonlight, gasping for air twenty feet away. His limbs were twitching, as if in a seizure. Perhaps a heart attack had already claimed him before the waves got their chance?

They pounded over his head again and she lost sight of him. She swam in his direction, buffeted about, then caught a glimpse of a raised hand. She had no idea how often he'd gone under. He seemed oblivious to everything, his body going through the automatic motions of struggling for life. When she reached him he didn't seem to know who she was or whether she was real. He kept trying to say a name that wasn't hers.

How she found the strength she didn't know, but Alison managed to swim behind him, pulling his head back, screaming for him to relax and just let his body float.

He thrashed about, with renewed life, fists flailing in the water as if trying to punch her. He twisted from her grasp and went under. She lost sight of him, then felt his torso crash into her legs, automatically grasping hold and pulling her down. She kicked out in terror until he let go. His body surfaced for a second and she saw that his jacket was gone, his shirt buttons burst open. She grabbed hold of his hair which felt like seaweed. It came loose and she grabbed a second handful, pulling him around until they were face to face. He seemed to know who she was now.

'Let me die, blast you, let me die!' She couldn't hear the words, just watched his mouth open and close. But she understood them and the fury in his eyes.

'I can't, fuck you, I can't.' She doubted if he could hear her over the waves. She'd never been this cold before, colder than death. Her teeth rattled, she felt about to be sick. Another wave came and they both went under, limbs frantically locked together, scrambling for something to hold. She came up and knew she couldn't carry on. Her rush of strength was gone. She almost blacked out, then, from her dream, that image of a submerged woman flashed before her. It frightened her into flailing out her arms, yet she didn't know if she could even reach the shore alone. Chris could sense the ebb within her too. She saw him try to swim for her sake, arms stupidly floundering around.

'Turn around,' she tried screaming, 'turn, you bastard.' No words came out, just more water rushing down her throat. But he seemed to understand and let himself go. At her mercy, at her trust. She tried to take deep breaths and not black out. She kicked out weakly, one arm around his neck, until eventually she knew she could kick no more. Her legs sank, touched sand and collapsed. A wave covered them, then rushed out, showering them in sand and pebbles. Chris staggered to his knees, then fell again. They were under water suddenly, another wave rolling them backwards.

Then Alison saw Sheila's face in her mind and she crawled to her knees. Hallucinatory images swamped her as she tried to stay conscious. She felt herself crawling past shards of floating glass, through a rusting porthole window, brushing against flitting shoals of rainbow fish. She fought against this pull towards unconsciousness, gripping Chris's hair, tearing at it, using the pain to lever him to his knees. Another wave washed over them but they had almost reached the shore. She panted like an animal, crawling on her hands and her knees, pulling him alone and scratching with her nails if he didn't crawl fast enough. Alison was crying. Sand clung to her face and hair as she sank down. Her body twitched and shivered and she was almost sick.

Chris lay beside her, face up, making a noise she couldn't fathom. They lay for an eternity, their bodies almost touching, and then his hand found hers and grasped it, his body rolling over so that he lay astride her. Her mouth was already open, yearning for the long-awaited taste of his tongue, before he kissed her. Yet it didn't feel sexual, it felt primeval, like the struggle to emerge from the water. The warmth of his tongue against hers, its urgent probing, its quest for something tangible, something made whole again.

Everything else tasted of sand and salt. The hotel seemed another world away. She had saved a life. Every muscle ached and yet amphetamines kept exploding throughout her body. She felt herself twelve, eighteen, she was every age and any age. Her sweatshirt was half torn, his shirt long gone. He raised his lips a second.

'Jesus,' he whispered, 'I wanted you so badly.'

She kissed him again, feeling renewed life in his limbs. His hands were in her hair, brushing her neck, touching her shoulders, sloping slowly down across her neck until suddenly they stopped. Chris lowered his head, then slowly rolled onto his side.

'In the waves I thought you were someone else,' he whispered, 'Jane come to meet me.'

Sand was everywhere, in her eyes, her bellybutton, her fanny. It seemed to course through her, mingled in her blood. All the water in the world would never shift it or rid her nostrils of this tang. The amphetamines were fading, leaving her body drained and wrecked, skin wrinkled by salt water, hair a tangled mess.

'I wanted to let you do it,' she said. 'I'd do the same myself.'

'Then why stop me?'

His tone was bitter now. She sensed his body shiver with shock and cold. Her neck was sore as if he had bruised it in withdrawing his hand.

'Would you have stopped me?'

'No.' he replied. 'Not if I knew what grief you were going through. What am I to do with the rest of my life?'

'I don't know. Start again. You said yourself you're free. A terrible freedom but free all the same.'

'How can I? I know who I was once, before Jane and the girls. But I can't bring him back and the person I became should have died in that car as well.'

'He didn't,' Alison insisted. 'You're still here.'

'Whose fault is that?' Anger had left his tone, there was just exhausted bewilderment. 'I would either be with them now or in oblivion where I wouldn't care.'

'You're lying if you say you wouldn't have stopped me too,' Alison said. 'Not if you'd one ounce of love left.'

Alison loved Peadar, she loved her children, but there was more to her than just them. Chris's naked chest was rising and falling, still fighting for breath.

'I've cursed you these last days,' he said, 'almost as much as I've longed for you. Just when I'd emptied my heart of everything you come back in. You knew me as a coward, but just this once I found the courage. Now I'm scared shitless. Not of death but of life. I'm scared of tomorrow and every day after.'

'You'll find someone else.'

'I wouldn't know how to start. I'm too old.'

'You're not.'

'Inside I am,' Chris said. 'All routes cut off. Two neat stitches in each testicle and that was the end of that.'

'They can reverse those operations,' she told him. 'It's not easy, but . . .'

'I don't want it reversed. I knew it was final. No matter if the sky fell on my head. Now the world tastes of cardboard, you understand? Nothing feels like it once did because part of me is dead. My taste buds. The nerve ends on my fingers.'

Chris turned towards her, his hand inches away.

'I can't leave my children any longer,' she said.

'No.'

'How do I know you won't . . .' she hesitated.

'Not tonight at least. I just want sleep. I've not slept properly for weeks. Taking comfort from planning this night. I wanted to die somewhere where I might feel close to them. I never expected to see you here.'

'Coincidences occur.'

'I'm not so sure.'

Alison backed away slightly from his gaze. 'I'm not the person you knew,' she said. 'Every year I come here I'm older, more battered inside. I didn't think I'd make it this year. I almost lost a breast.'

She was telling him details she had withheld from Peadar. She should feel guilty lying here, but she did not.

'You're the same woman you ever were,' Chris replied. He was close to her again but she didn't back away. Her eyes closed as she felt his hand touch her stomach, drawing the torn sweatshirt slowly up until, after what seemed an eternity, he touched her nipple. Chris's hand felt like she had always known it would. Unhurried, gentle, the first man to touch her breast in fifteen years, apart from Peadar and Dr O'Gorman. The only man ever, apart from Peadar really. The others didn't count, their hands had left no trace, and even now, under Chris's touch, the spell of Dr O'Gorman's cold fingers, which had made her fear her own breasts, seemed banished.

How long was it since she had felt this young, her nipple erect, straining against the ghost of intricate red stitching? Chris's fingers circled, savouring its fullness, the ripeness of a young orange plucked. The tang of sea air. Alison kept her eyes shut, knowing his were closed as well. He brushed tenderly against the stitch, then his hand went still, cradling her nipple between thumb and finger. Five seconds, fifteen, twenty. How long did two decades take? She opened her eyes.

'Thank you,' he said, slowly withdrawing his hand. Both knew that anything more between them would be mundane and superfluous.

Neither spoke as they picked themselves up and climbed the steps. A few late drinkers remained in the Slaney Room, where light spilled out onto the patio. Chris took her hand and she followed along the dark boardwalk, through bushes and shadows, the hidden ripple of water, lamps casting shadows. They reached the tennis courts and she almost broke loose, desperate to check her children.

She opened the French doors and pushed the curtain aside. All three slept on, though Danny had turned over, with his giraffe fallen onto the floor. She wanted to run in and hug them, but every inch of her skin was plastered in sand. Her body shivered with a foretaste of pneumonia. Gravel stung her bare feet. Life felt different, every sensation magnified. Only now was shock properly taking hold. Chris let go her hand gently and stepped back, away from her.

'I'd forgotten what life tasted like.'

'So had I.'

'I'll make no promises,' he said. 'Still, I'm starting to miss that blasted dog.'

They didn't kiss or touch again. She watched him slowly walk to his own room, looking back just once to raise a hand in thanks or farewell.

When she closed the French doors, her legs almost gave way. She made the shower so hot it scorched her skin. But she didn't care. Alison leaned forward beneath it, holding onto the tiled wall with both hands. The water coursed through her hair and down her back, splashing over her belly and breasts, yet still could not remove the feel of his hand. She turned the shower off and dried herself.

The children were sleeping. She let her robe fall, placed Danny's giraffe back beside him and walked naked towards the bed. When had she last felt this special? It was a secret she would never speak of, to Ruth or to the man she loved. Except maybe to Sheila in many years' time.

She could see so clearly now. Sleep was needed because her lover would be here in the morning for her. The car to be loaded and farewells said, though Chris would long be gone. Enniscorthy, then Gorey and Ferns, the motorway beyond Arklow, the mountains rising, then falling as they plummeted towards Rathnew and Ashford. Every mile bringing them closer, causing the chorus of voices from the back seat to call, 'Are we there yet, Mammy, are we home?'

# ABOUT THE AUTHOR

Dermot Bolger is the author of six novels (including *The Journey Home* and *Father's Music*), seven plays and several volumes of poetry. He devised, edited and co-wrote the best-selling collaborative novel *Finbar's Hotel*, and its sequel *Ladies' Night at Finbar's Hotel*, and is also the editor of the *New Picador Book of Contemporary Irish Fiction*.